# Tales of the Texians

By Dorothy Tutt Sinclair

Dorothy Sinclair Enterprises, Bellaire, Texas

Tales of the Texians
by Dorothy Tutt Sinclair

Illustrations
by Harris Milam

Book Design
by Francine Mangus

FIRST EDITION

Copyright © 1985 by Dorothy Tutt Sinclair

Published in the United States of America
by Dorothy Sinclair Enterprises,
P.O. Box 782, Bellaire, Texas 77401-0782

Library of Congress Catalog Card Number  85-90411
ISBN 0-9615311-1-8

# *Tales of the Texians*
## Table of Contents

# *Tales of the Texians*
## Illustrations

# The Six Flags of Texas

Have you ever crossed from one state to another on an interstate highway? If you have, you might have seen a building called a Visitors' Center. That is where you can find out about the places and people of that state. Its flag along with that of the United States flies in front of the building.

When a person comes to Texas he will have a hard time missing the Visitors' Center. He will see six flags in front of the building. Do you know why? It's because six countries have flown their flags over Texas to show it belonged to them.

There is no flag for the people who lived on this land for the longest time. They were Indians. For thousand of years Indian families and tribes lived here. Some were farmers. Others were hunters or fishermen. A few tribes were traders. They moved about swapping animal skins or flint for food and other things they needed. There was no flag over the land until the white man came.

In 1492 when Columbus discovered America, he claimed this "new world" for Spain. It was not until 1519 that a man named Pineda discovered Texas. He sailed along the Gulf of Mexico and made a map of the coast. He also stopped to trade with the Indians. He raised the first Spanish flag over this land. The Spanish Flag is red and white with red lions and golden castles on it. Pineda called this land Amichel.

Later other Spaniards carried the flag of Spain to Texas. Most of the men were soldiers looking for gold and riches. The Indians had never seen white men nor horses before. Some Indians were friendly. Others tried to kill the Spaniards. They feared and hated the white men, but they wanted their horses!

Other nations wanted to own land in the "new world." France sent people to live in the North in Canada. They raised the flag of France there. The French flag has golden lilies called "fleur-de-lis" (flŏor-də-lé) on a field of white. The French made friends with the Indians and traded with them for furs. One Frenchman named La Salle floated down the Mississippi River. He planted the French flag at the edge of the Gulf of Mexico. Because of this, France claimed all the land that drained into that mighty river.

La Salle asked the King of France to give him ships and supplies. He wanted to start a colony near the mouth of the Mississippi River. He set out with four ships and four hundred people, but his plan did not work. One ship was taken by the Spanish. One ship was wrecked. The third ship turned back to France with many people and supplies. La Salle himself missed the mouth of the Mississippi River. Instead, in February, 1685, La Salle landed in Texas on the shore of Matagorda Bay. He and his men built a fort which they named Fort St. Louis in honor of the French King. The French flag became the second to wave over Texas.

When the King of Spain learned about Fort St. Louis, he sent soldiers and priests from Mexico. The priests wanted to build missions for the Indians. The King ordered his soldiers to watch the French and look after the missions. In this way Spain could have its people living in Texas, too.

For a long time both France and Spain claimed Texas. Many years later France sold the Louisiana Territory to the United States. Some Americans thought Texas was part of the deal, but Spain still claimed the land. At last, when Spain gave up Florida, a line was drawn that gave Texas to Spain, but not for long.

In 1810 the people living in Mexico began to fight for freedom from Spain. Texas was part of Mexico. In 1821 when Mexico won, a new green, white, and red flag waved over Texas. On the middle bar of the Mexican Flag is an eagle sitting on a cactus, holding a snake in its mouth. This flag was number three.

The Spanish rulers had not wanted people from the United States to live in Texas. The new Mexican leaders agreed to let Americans in. Mexico let a few men called empresarios sell land. Moses and Stephen F. Austin were the first empresarios (ām-prā-sä-rĭ-ōs) in Texas. The people who bought the land had to follow laws of Mexico.

At first all went well. Then Mexico wrote new laws that were bad for Texas. The settlers did not obey the new laws so Mexico sent soldiers to Texas. This led to war. It ended with a great victory for Texas at the Battle of San Jacinto. Under its leaders in 1836, Texas became a free country called the Republic of Texas.

Each nation's flag is the sign or symbol that stands for that country. Each thinks its flag is the best. Many Texans, like Stephen F. Austin, had ideas how the Texas flag should look. Lorenzo de Zavala (lō-rāń-sō dā sä-vä́-lä) wanted the letters T-E-X-A-S between the five points of a white star on a blue field. David Burnet wanted the star to be gold, not white. Another design became the flag of the Republic of Texas. It has a white band over a red band with a blue bar on the side. In the center of the blue bar is a white star. It is a flag that has always made Texans proud.

In 1846 Texas became a part of the United States. The American flag had thirteen red and white stripes with a white star on blue for each state. Texas became the twenty-eighth star on Old Glory. The beautiful flag of the Republic of Texas became the state flag.

Texas joined the United States because it was better for the people to be a part of that strong union. Yet in a few years all the states in the South left the Union to form the Confederacy. Texas left, also. This brought on the "War Between the States." That is when the sixth flag flew over Texas.

The Confederate battle flag was red with blue stripes crossing from the corners. Thirteen white stars were placed on the blue stripes. At the end of the war, all the states which had left joined the Union again.

Today there are two flags that wave over Texas. Texans are proud of both – the flag of the United States and the flag of this great State. People everywhere in the world know about Texas and its flag. Because of its one white star on its blue bar, Texas is called the Lone Star State. The flag is a sign of the brave and friendly people who live here. It calls to mind the bigness and richness of its land. The flag is a symbol of hope. It has brought many people here to make their homes. They, too, love Texas. They are proud to be Texans living in a land that has been under six flags.

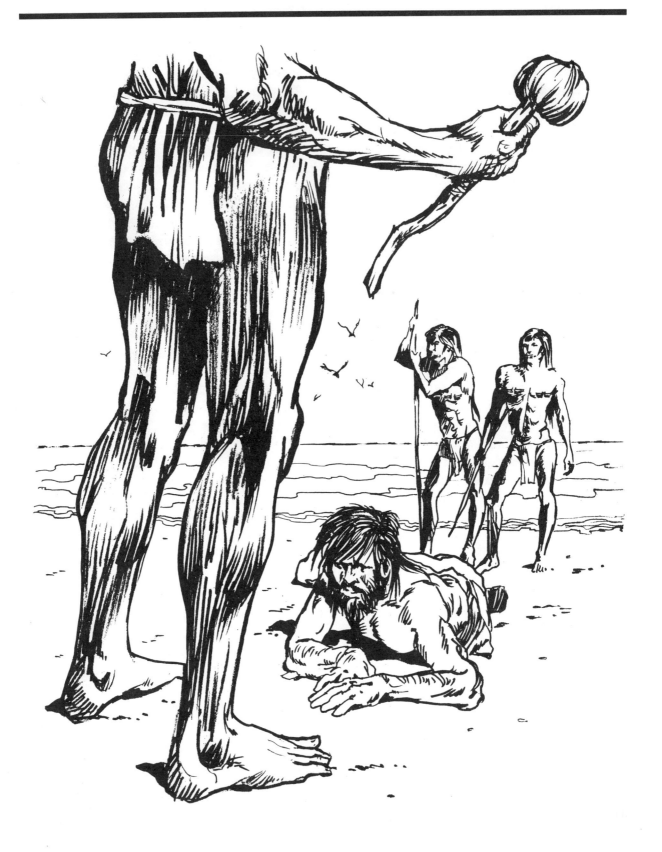

# *Indians*

If you were going to a strange planet, what kinds of things would you want to know? You'd surely want to know if any people lived there and how they would look. Would they be friends or enemies? Would you be able to talk to them and understand them? What kind of food would they eat? Would there be animals on the planet and what kind? So many questions you would have!

The first white men who came to Texas must have asked themselves the same questions. It did not take long to find out that there were people living here. The white men called them Indians, but the Indians were not all alike. Some were friendly but others were not. Some lived in one place while others moved about. Even the food they ate and where they got it was different.

Cabeza de Vaca was one of the first men to tell about Texas Indians. He was part of a group who came from Spain looking for gold. The Spaniards landed in 1528 in Florida, but were driven away from there by Indians. While they were on land, the ships on which they had come sailed away to Cuba. The men made boats of logs and horsehides to try to sail to Mexico. On the way a storm wrecked the boats on the coast of Texas. Most of the men drowned. A few were washed up on the shore of an island. They called the island "Malhado." Its name today is Galveston.

Cabeza de Vaca (kä-bā-ŝ dā vä-́kä) and three men were washed upon the shore. One man was black. His name was Estevanico, or Stephen. When the men woke up, they found Karankawa (kä-rănǵ-kä-wä) Indians standing around them.

The Karankawas (kä-răng'-kä-wä) were tall, strong Indians who were cruel. They lived along the coast where they hunted and fished for food. They ate crabs, snails, oysters, fish, and alligators. They painted their bodies and put on smelly fish oils to keep mosquitos away. The Karankawas did not live together as a tribe, but sometimes families joined to fight enemies. They either killed their enemies and ate their flesh or kept them as slaves. They watched the slaves all the time and were very mean to them.

Cabeza de Vaca and his friends were made slaves. They worked without stopping from sunup to sundown. Whenever the Karankawas moved, the slaves took down and put up their houses. The houses were made of poles covered with skins or reeds.

How the Spaniards wanted to escape! They watched for a chance, but years passed before they were able to get away. Cabeza de Vaca and his friends planned to walk to Mexico so they headed west. Imagine how they felt when they were taken almost at once by other Indians! These Indians, the Coahuiltecans, made the Spaniards slaves, too. These Indians were like the Karankawas in many ways, but they were not so cruel.

The Coahuitecans (kō-́ä-wēl-́tĕ-käns) moved about in bands looking for food. They lived in small houses made of four hoops covered with mats of grass. Where they lived was almost a desert. Only cactus and dry brush grew there. There were few animals to eat. The Coahuiltacans ate spiders, lizards, rattlesnakes, and roots. They were nearly always hungry.

In the fall many of the Coahuiltecan bands came together. They gathered nuts and the fruit of the cactus called "prickly pear." They traded shells, rocks, and things they had made. They danced and had feasts. They also brought sick Indians to the Medicine Man. He did strange things to make them well.

Cabeza de Vaca saw how important the Medicine Man was to the Indians. He was free to go from one tribe to another. Cabeza de Vaca decided to become a Medicine Man. He tried to help the sick and he prayed to God for them. Because the Indians got well, he and his friends were able to be free. At last they started to Mexico. After almost eight years they reached the end of their travel.

Cabeza de Vaca wrote a book about all that had happened. People learned about the land and the Indians who lived in one part of Texas. At the same time, Indians who lived in East Texas were very different.

## THE FOREST INDIANS

The Indians who lived in the forest lands were peace-loving people. There were many tribes. Each had its chief, but the tribes belonged to a "Confederation." The Great Chief of the Confederation was called the "Caddi." They also had a high priest called "Xinesi." He kept a flame burning all the time in the Great Caddi Temple.

The Wichita Indians lived along the Red River in the North Central part of Texas. The Hasinai (hă-sĭ-nī´) and the Caddos (kăd-´ōs) made their home in East Texas in the forest. Each tribe lived in a village.

The Caddos lived in houses that looked like beehives. They planted trees in a circle and joined the branches together at the top. Other branches, grasses, and leaves covered the tree house to keep out the wind and rain. Inside there were mats on the floor. They slept on beds on poles with buffalo skins for cover.

The Caddos lived by farming. They planted two kinds of corn, beans, squash, pumpkins, sun flowers, and tobacco. They also had peach, plum, fig, and chestnut trees. Both the men and the women worked in the fields. Sometimes the men went hunting, but this was not needed for everyday food.

Caddo women cooked and made clothes. The clothes were made of deer skin. They worked with the skins until they were soft and shiny as silk. They painted the skins with bright colors and sewed seeds and shells on them. The women also made bowls of clay and baskets of grass. These things made their homes beautiful.

The Caddo men were kind to their wives and children. They were good neighbors and liked to have company. When strangers came, the Caddos had a feast for them and gave them presents. Strangers did not always understand that the Caddos were glad to see them. You see, the Caddos cried and howled sadly to show they were happy!

The Caddos did not like to fight and make war. The name of one of their tribes was Tejas (tā-́häs). That word means "friend" in the language of the Caddos. Because the Tejas were friendly to the first Spanish priests, they called this land Texas.

THE HUNTERS

The Hill Country is west of the forest lands toward the middle of Texas. This is where the Tonkawa Indians made their home because deer and antelope were found there. The Tonkawas were great hunters who lived on deer meat.

The name Tonkawa means "they all stay together." They lived in small villages in houses made of willow sticks covered with skins. The men hunted together and brought the deer back to the village. If the hunt was good, they had a feast and danced and sang. If the hunt was bad, they were all hungry together.

The Tonkawa women cleaned and worked with deer skins. They made clothes from the skins while the men made arrow points and spears with flint rock which they found along streams. This rock was very sharp. Other Indians wanted flint for arrows and sharp tools, too. They also wanted deer skins to make clothes. The Tonkawas traded with other Indians to get food and things they needed.

The Indians who lived on the Plains were hunters, too. They hunted the buffalo or bison. Buffalo wandered over the plains in great herds. No one knows how many millions there were. In the spring the buffalo came to eat the sweet grass. As the sun grew hotter, the herds went north. In the fall the bison came again.

The Apaches (à-păch-́ēz) and the Comanches (kō-măn-́chēs) lived on the buffalo. They ate his flesh and used his hide for clothes and cover. They used his bones to make tools and spoons. They also made bow strings, belts, and ropes from the buffalo. Whatever the reason, whether it was because hunting was full of danger or because they simply liked to kill, the Apaches and the Comanches were the most feared and hated Indians in Texas.

Bands of Apaches, Mescaleros and Lipan-Apaches followed the buffalo on the Texas Plains. They lived in tepees of buffalo skins that could be moved very quickly. The Apaches used dogs to pull a sledge called a "travois" (trə-voi´) to carry the tepees. The Apache women and children went everywhere with the hunters. They cooked and dried buffalo meat and worked with the hides. If a brave had no woman, he would steal one to work for him.

The Apaches could hunt buffalo only in the spring and fall. They learned to plant beans, maise, squash, and pumpkin. Bands of Apaches made camp and planted crops along the rivers and streams. The Spanish called these Apache camps "rancherias."

The Apaches liked to fight as much as to hunt. They fought and stole from Indians as well as the white man. The name Apache means "enemy."

The Apaches, although very fierce and mean, did fear another tribe – the Comanches. The Comanches were small in size, but they were the greatest horsemen in the world. They stole horses from the Spanish and learned to control them. The Spanish mustang was strong and fast. It liked living on the plains. The Comanches made bridles and bits from buffalo hide, but they rode without a saddle. They rode as if the horse and rider were one. On the back of a horse, every Comanche was a chief.

Like the Apaches, the Comanches lived by killing buffalo but they were never hungry. On horseback they could follow the buffalo wherever they went. Like the Apaches, the Comanches liked to fight. They could strike the enemy and ride away before they were attacked. The Comanches and their families lived on horseback, not in villages.

The Comanches did one thing no other horsemen had done. They learned to drop over the side of their horses while they were running very fast. They then could shoot arrows or a gun from under the horse's head!

There are many stories about the Apaches and the Comanches, In the 1800's many white people came to Texas. Most were farmers who lived far from neighbors. Apaches or Comanches often stole their horses or cattle. Sometimes they killed the people or took them away. One child the Comanches took was named Cynthia Ann Parker.

Cynthia Ann lived with her family and about twenty people in a fort. She was nine years old when the Comanches attacked. They killed the men but took Cynthia Ann, her brother, and three other people. Sometimes the Indians sold the people they had taken to another tribe or to white men. The Comanches did not sell Cynthia Ann and her brother. They became part of the Comanche tribe.

Cynthia Ann had blond hair and blue eyes. She was seen or heard of many times. When she grew up, she married Peta Nacona (nō-kō´nä). He was the Chief of the Naconi band of Comanches. They had two sons, Pecos and Quanah (kwă´nä) and a little girl named Prairie Flower.

When Cynthia Ann was thirty-four years old, her life changed again. Peta Nacona led a war party back near the place where Cynthia Ann had been taken. Some Texas Rangers followed the Comanches. They found a camp where the Comanche women and children were waiting for their braves. One Ranger saw Cynthia Ann's blue eyes and dirty blond hair. They took her and her baby girl back with them.

Cynthia Ann could speak no English. She said her name was Naduah, but her family knew she was Cynthia Ann. They tried to do all they could for her but she was never happy. She had lived too long as a Comanche. She missed her husband and her sons. When Prairie Flower was four years old, she died. Cynthia Ann acted like an Indian mother. She no longer wanted to live. She prayed to the Great Spirit. Then she starved herself to death.

Quanah Parker, the son of Cynthia Ann and Chief Peta Nacona, was the last of the great Comanche chiefs. The Comanches were having hard times because white hunters killed most of the buffalo. There were many fights between the Indians and the Texans. The Texas Rangers tried to guard the settlers. The United States army also fought the Comanches. The Comanches would

attack and then disappear on the plains. No one knew where they went. At last the army found out. The Comanches were camping in Palo Duro Canyon.

One night soldiers went single file down into the canyon They stampeded the Comanches' horses and set fire to the Indians' supplies. The Comanches were helpless to fight back. Without their horses, the Comanches could not fight! The end had come!

All the Indians in Texas were rounded up. Many tribes had disappeared. Some had been killed by the white man or other Indians. Others had fallen to an enemy they could not see. The sickness that killed the white man also killed the Indian. A few Indians were from tribes that had been pushed off their land and into Texas. They had no place of their own. It was a sad time for all red men.

The United States set aside lands for the Indians. These lands were called "reservations." The Indians in Texas were told that they must go to a reservation in Oklahoma. They could never come back to Texas. They looked to their leader Quanah Parker. He knew they had to go, so he led them to Oklahoma.

The story of the Indians is a sad one. When the settlers came to America, they wanted land. Sometimes they traded the Indians for it. Most of the time they did not ask. They cleared the forest, built houses and planted seeds. Some Indians moved on, but many wanted to keep their land. Often there was a fight. If the Indian won, other white men were afraid for their families. If the white man won, the Indians hated him for two reasons. He had taken the land and killed their people.

As the Americans moved west, the Indians were pushed ahead of them. The Cherokee, Delaware, Osage, Choctaw, Alabama, Coushatta and Seminole tribes were pushed into Texas. Many of them went on to other places but the Alabama and Coushatta tribes stayed.

They were much like the Caddos. They farmed, fished and hunted in East Texas, but it happened again! As more white settlers came to Texas, they pushed the Alabama Indians off the land. Sam Houston, who was a friend to the Indians, gave the Alabama-Coushatta a reservation. It is near Livingston in the Big Thicket. There is another Indian reservation in Texas near El Paso. The Tiqua Indians who came from New Mexico live at Isleta where a mission once stood.

Not all Indians were bad, nor all white men good. Both made mistakes and then bad things happened. Both wanted the same land. Neither tried to understand the other. The priests tried to show the Indians love and ways of peace. They wanted the Indians to live like the white man. But the Indians wanted to be free to live as their people had lived before them. They did not want farms and fences on the land.

Both the white man and the Indian were brave. They fought for what they thought was theirs. In the end the strongest won. Does that mean it was right? What do you think?

## *The Legend of the Bluebonnet*

Long ago there was a time when the Great Spirit was angry with the Indian. He sent mighty floods that washed away the land. He made the sun very hot and baked the earth. Then he froze the plains with snow and icy winds.

The people and animals could find no food to eat. There was much suffering. Many grew sick and died. It was a time of great sadness.

The Comanche Chief called his people together. They came to the council fire to seek help. The wise men, the medicine men and the shaman, spoke together.

"You must pray unto the Great Spirit," they told the Chief.

All knelt to pray, each with his family.

The Comanche Chief prayed long and hard for his people. At last there was a voice.

"You must burn that which you love the most. Scatter the ashes to the four winds. Then there will be an end to your suffering."

The people rose to their feet. Each brave and his family went to his tepee. They had suffered so much. Did the Great Spirit want them to suffer more? Their sorrow grew deeper and deeper.

The Comanche Chief had a little daughter. She had heard her father pray. She also heard the Voice. She was very sad. She picked up her doeskin doll to hold tight. The doll had a bonnet made of blue feathers. The little girl thought it was the most beautiful doll in the world. She loved it more than anything she owned.

That night the little Indian girl could not sleep. Somehow she knew that she must help her people. If she burned her doll, the thing she loved most, would the Great Spirit help them?

Very quietly the little Indian girl slipped out of the tepee. She went to the campfire and took a red coal from it. She carried the coal and bits of wood to a bare hill nearby. There she made a fire and laid her doll on the flames. Through her tears she saw her doll turn to ashes. Then she prayed to the Great Spirit for her people.

The little Indian girl waited until the fire went out. She took the ashes and scattered them to the four winds. She put dirt over the place where the fire had been. In the dark she felt something soft under her fingers. She could not pick it up. It was fastened to the ground.

The next morning the hillside was covered with bright blue flowers. They were the color of the doll's feather bonnet. Everyone wondered at the sight.

The Comanche asked the wise ones what had happened. They said someone had obeyed the words of the Great Spirit. The Chief asked each brave if he had left his tepee during the night. All shook their heads.

At last the little girl told her father what she had done. How proud of her he was, for her bravery! She had saved her people. This was a sign from the Great Spirit all would be well.

Every spring blue flowers bloom on the hills of Texas. They are called "bluebonnets". They are a gift from the Comanche. The bluebonnet is the state flower of Texas.

## The Missions

When Columbus discovered America, he brought back to Spain things he had found in the new country. He brought parrots, plants, cotton, gold, and people he called Indians. The King of Spain was very pleased because he wanted gold for his country. The soldiers saw the "new world" as a place where they could get rich. The priests saw the Indians as people who needed to know about God. Everyone was excited! It was not long before many ships sailed west with soldiers and priests.

Wherever the soldiers went, the priests went too. The soldiers took the land from the Indians and were cruel to them. The priests gave love to the Indians and were kind to them. The soldiers made the Indians work very hard and killed thousands of them. The priests worked with the Indians to make their lives better. The soldiers wanted gold and silver for themselves. The priests wanted to build churches to please God. The sword and the Cross went together, but how different were the reasons! The Indians did not know what to think.

Cabeza de Vaca and Esteban came looking for gold. They never found it, but they heard of the Seven Cities of Gold. Cibola (sē-́bō-lä) was said to be the largest and richest. Fray Marcos asked Esteban to go with him to find Cibola. When Esteban went to talk to the Indians in Cibola, they killed him. Fray Marcos was afraid to go to Cibola. He only saw it from far away but he was sure it was made of gold.

Because of the stories of Cabeza de Vaca and Fray Marcos, Coronado set out for Cibola. He led over three hundred soldiers, one thousand Indians, and three priests. For almost two years they looked, but there were no cities of gold. There were only Indian villages made of mud.

Whether it was because there was no gold or because Texas was so big, for one hundred fifty years Spain forgot about Texas.

A man named La Salle brought some French people to live in Texas. They landed at Matagorda Bay and built a fort there. They called the fort St. Louis after the French king. By living on the land, they said it belonged to France.

When the King of Spain heard about Fort St. Louis, he did not like it. He sent Captain de Leon and Father Massanet (mäs-sä-nä´) to find it. Before they arrived, La Salle had been killed. Many of the French settlers had died from sickness and Indians had killed most of the others. Captain de Leon and Father Massanet went further east. They wanted to see if other Frenchmen were there. They found no French but they met friendly Indians – the Tejas. Their chief asked Father Massanet about the white man's god. He asked Father Massanet to teach his people about God. Father Massanet promised to come back in a year and build a mission.

The priests had asked the King of Spain many times to let them set up missions. This time the King agreed. He wanted priests and soldiers in Texas. He felt this would keep the French and other people away.

True to his word, Father Massanet came back in a year. He built a church of logs and a house for the priests and soldiers. This was the first mission in Texas. It was called San Francisco de los Tejas. San Francisco means "Saint

Francis." De los Tejas shows that it was built for the Tejas Indians. Three priests and three soldiers stayed at the mission. The priests were to teach the Indians about God and the church. The soldiers were to guard the priests.

At first all went well. Most of the Indians liked the priests, but the medicine men hated them. The soldiers began to do bad things to the Indians. Many of the Indians became sick and the medicine men told all of them to stay away from the mission. Then the food supply ran out. The priests and soldiers went back to Mexico.

Another small mission was built in East Texas. It was called Santisimo Nombre de Maria. It was washed away in a flood about one year later. This was not a very good beginning for missions in Texas.

Almost twenty years passed before another mission was started. The French again made Spain build missions in Texas. The French were trading with Indians along the Red and Sabine Rivers. Spain was afraid this would cause trouble with the Indians. The priests were glad to try once more to set up missions.

Missions were built a second time in East Texas near where the first had been. There were five altogether. They were named San Francisco de Los Neches, Nuestra Senora de Guadalupe, Nuestra Senora de Delores, La Purisima Concepcion, and San Jose de los Nazones. To guard all five missions, a fort was built at Delores. A sixth mission, San Miguel de Linares, was built in Louisiana.

No matter how hard they tried, the priests could not get the Indians to live in the missions. The crops failed and some

of the soldiers left. The French marched on Mission San Miguel de Linares in Louisiana. They took it. Then word came that the French were on their way to Texas. The priests left in great fear. The missions were too far away from Mexico to get help when they needed it.

About the same time another mission was started. It was five hundred miles closer to Mexico on the Camino Real, or King's Highway. The mission was called San Antonio de Valero, but we know it today as the Alamo. A presidio, San Antonio de Bexar, was built close by, near San Pedro Spring. This was a place where travelers to Louisiana or Mexico liked to stop and rest.

The land around San Antonio de Valero was perfect for a mission. There was good water in the river and springs, and trees along the banks. The land was rich for growing food with plenty of grass for horses and cattle. Fish from the streams and game were easy to get. It was not long before other missions were built nearby. San Jose de Aguayo was about "two gunshots" away from San Antonio de Valero. Three missions from East Texas moved further down the San Antonio River. These were San Francisco de Espada, Concepcion, and San Juan Capistrano.

The priests learned many things from missions that failed. They knew that a mission had to be part church, part fort, and part town. The first building was always the church. While the Indians helped build it, the priests told them about God. The church was made with strong walls so it could be a fort, too. There had to be houses for the priests, Indians, and soldiers in which to live. The

ALAMO MISSION

houses needed to be close to the church within thick walls to keep the people inside safe. There had to be places to make and store all the things that the people needed.

San Jose de Aguaya was built just as the priests wanted all missions built. It was laid out like a big square. The walls were made of stone and were very high. Along three sides there were eighty-four apartments where the Indians lived. On the fourth side the priests and soldiers had their houses. Inside the walls the church and other buildings stood. There were gates at the four corners of the mission and one in front of the church. There were holes in the walls near the gates through which they could shoot enemies. The gates were opened only twice a day. In the morning they let Indians out to work in the fields and tend the cattle. In the afternoon they were opened to let the Indians back inside.

Everyone in the mission worked. The Indian women wove cloth, made clothes, cooked for their families, and kept house.

The Indian men built buildings, made furniture, learned to work with tools, ground corn, and did other jobs. The children went to school. All learned about God and the church.

Many Indians did not like to work. They were lazy and dirty. They wanted only the food and the pretty things the priests gave them. They liked to hunt and fish and go wherever they wanted to go. Many came to the mission to get away from their enemies. Yet the priests kept on trying to teach them about God and to save them.

Running a mission took many skills. A priest needed to know how to do everything to be able to teach the Indians. He had to know how to build walls and houses; to farm and raise animals; to grind, store, and cook food. He needed to know how to spin and weave cloth. He had to be able to care for sick people and to make things he needed that he did not have. He must do all these things while he was doing the one thing he had come to do – to teach the Indians about God. He had to bring Indians to the mission and keep them there. He had to keep records of all the Indians who came to the Mission and joined the church.

There were twenty-one missions in East Texas that are known about. La Bahia mission and fort were built where Fort St. Louis had stood. The mission was moved two times – first to Victoria and then to Goliad. Several small missions were built on the San Saba River. They were for the Apaches who wanted to be safe from the Comanches. The last mission was called Nuestra Senora de Refugio, Our Lady of Refuge.

For almost a hundred years the priest ran the missions. Some failed because there were too few soldiers to guard them. Others failed because the Indians would not live within the mission walls. A few were lost to storms while the Indians burned others. At last there were so few Indians in the missions that the rulers decided to close them. The priests divided the land, the animals, and the tools among the Indians. If the mission was near a town, the church was given to the people who lived there. If not, the building just stood alone. It must have been a very sad time for the priests. Had all their work been for nothing? They must have thought so, but we know differently.

There are still missions in Texas. It is true that the Indians have gone, but the buildings still stand. They are signs of the work, the bravery, and the love of the priests. Mission San Jose de Aguayo in San Antonio is a place where you can see the priests' plan. It is one of the most beautiful missions in America. You can visit Goliad and see a church that has moved three times and still lives. And you can go to the Alamo where brave men gave their lives for Texas. Perhaps the most important work of the missions was not to save the Indians. Perhaps it was to make us remember the people and their dreams that have made Texas great.

# Jane Long

Do you know what a promise is? Of course you do. It means that you say you will or will not do something. If you do not keep your promise, people will not trust you. But you must think carefully before you make a promise! This is a story about a promise and the brave lady who made it.

In 1803 the United States bought Louisiana from France. Nobody knew how much land Louisiana covered to the east and west. Many Americans thought Texas was part of the land deal, but Spain said she owned Texas. In 1819 the United States agreed with Spain. This made people angry. Some of them wanted to take Texas from Spain. They asked Dr. James Long to be their leader.

Dr. Long was a doctor, a soldier, a farmer, and a store keeper. He lived in Natches, Mississippi with his wife Jane and their little girl Ann. They had a happy life but Dr. Long had a dream. He wanted to start a new free country in Texas so he agreed to be the leader. He started for Nacogdoches with about seventy-five men. Before he reached Texas, there were three hundred men with him.

Jane Long was proud of her husband, but she hated to see him go. She wanted to be with him. Soon after he left, Jane had another baby. When the baby was two weeks old, Jane started to Texas to join Dr. Long. On the way Jane got sick. She stayed with her sister in Louisiana for a month. Then she started again for Texas. She left the baby with her sister, but she took Ann and a black maid named Kian with her. This time Jane reached Nacogdoches.

Dr. Long and his men captured Nacog-

doches. They told the people living there that they were free from Spain. Then they drew up papers to start the Republic of Texas. The men made Dr. Long the president.

Dr. Long knew that Spain would want Texas back. He sent most of the men away to four places to set up forts and trading posts. He went to Galveston Island to see Jean Lafitte, the pirate. Dr. Long wanted to get Lafitte to help him fight the Spanish. The pirate would not agree.

If Dr. Long's plans had worked, Jane would have been the "First Lady" of Texas. While Dr. Long was at Galveston Island, the Spanish army marched on Nacogdoches and took it. Dr. Long's men were driven out of Texas. Some people were killed but Jane, Ann, and Kian got to Louisiana safely. Dr. Long escaped to Louisiana, but he did not give up his dream.

In 1821 Dr. Long came back to Texas. He sailed from New Orleans to Galveston Island with soldiers and their families. Jane, Ann, and Kian went, too. The men built a fort on Bolivar Point on the mainland across from Galveston Island.

Dr. Long had learned that the people in Mexico were fighting to be free of Spain. He and about fifty men went to Goliad to take the town. He left soldiers at the fort to look after Jane and the others. Dr. Long asked Jane not to leave the fort. The Karankawa Indians were on Galveston Island. Dr. Long said he would be back soon so Jane promised to wait for him. It was not far to Goliad. Dr. Long left on September 19, 1821.

During the warm September days, Jane and Ann walked along the beach.

They picked up shells and watched the sand crabs dig holes. They heard the waves gently lapping against the shore. They saw the gulls dive into the sea to catch silver fish in their beaks. Only a few days, Jane thought happily, until Dr. Long would be back.

The days added up to one week and then another. The winds grew sharp and the rains came. Everyone looked harder for the sight of a sail coming from the west. There was not one to be seen.

At the end of a month the soldiers talked among themselves. They felt sure Dr. Long and his men would have come back if they could. Something had happened. Either the men had been taken or they had been killed. They waited a few days before they spoke to Jane. Jane told the soldiers she was sure her husband would be back soon. There could be many reasons why the men were not back. She asked them to wait, too.

The fort had been built so quickly that it was not a very good place to live. The supplies which Dr. Long had left were getting low. Often the soldiers brought fish or game for supper.

As the days dragged on, the soldiers grew more restless. They had no hope of Dr. Long's coming back. They knew that if the Spanish army came, they could not hold out against it. They asked Jane to let them take her away so she could be looked after. Jane thanked them but she shook her head. She had promised her husband that she would wait for him. She must keep her promise.

The soldiers were very sad. They felt sorry for Jane, but they could not wait any longer. One by one they slipped away from the fort. At last there were only three persons left—Jane, Ann, and Kian.

At night Jane saw fires burning on Galveston Island. That meant Karankawa Indians were there. Every day Jane loaded the cannon and fired it. She hoped the Indians would think there were soldiers at the fort. She needed a flag to raise over the wall, but there was none. What could she use? She thought and thought. At last she found something bright and brave. She flew her red flannel petticoat!

With every passing day things grew worse. Icy winds screamed about the fort. The bay froze over. The skies opened and snow and sleet beat on the fort. The supplies of food were all gone. The only food was fish frozen in the waters of the bay. Kian grew sick and Jane could do little to make her well. Then on December 21, Jane gave birth to a baby girl. It was the first American child born in Texas.

With the coming of spring, living grew easier. For this Jane was glad but her heart was very sad. She knew something terrible had happened to her husband, but what could she do? She had no way to leave the fort if she had wanted to go. Where could she go to find out about Dr. Long? She must wait out her promise.

The days and weeks seemed like years. At last in July, Jane saw a small boat coming toward her. In it were two men. Were they Indians? How happy Jane was to see they were old friends, James and Randall Jones. They had come to take her to her sister's home. Once before, they had taken her to Louisiana when the Spanish took Nacogdoches. This time they had brought sad news. Dr. Long had been taken to Mexico and he had been killed. There was no need to wait out her promise.

You might think that Jane Long would never want to see Texas again. She had lost her husband and the baby she had left with her sister. She had no home of her own and no one to look after her. She had two small children to raise. But Jane Long had shared her husband's dream. She knew that Texas was a land of greatness. She wanted to be a part of it. When Stephen F. Austin made land grants to Americans, Jane was one of the first

three hundred to come.

In 1824 Jane went to San Felipe, but she soon moved to Brazoria. This was where many settlers stopped on the way to their land. With the help of people like Ben Milam, Jane had a house built. She let tired travelers come to her home, where they could rest and eat good food. She ran a boarding house where many of the leaders of Texas came to know her. In this way she earned a living for herself and her children.

A few years later Jane moved to Richmond. With Kian she opened up another boarding house. It, too, was successful. People enjoyed being with Jane. She was a lovely lady with a bright mind. Many important dinners, parties, and meetings were held at Jane's boarding house.

Jane never married although she was asked many times. Some thought she would have married Ben Milam if he had not been killed at the Battle of San Antonio. Mirabeau B. Lamar, the second president of the Republic of Texas, wrote poems to her. She was a good friend of Stephen F. Austin and other leaders. But Jane lived alone on her land grant just outside of Richmond. Kian or one of Kian's children always looked after her. Jane died when she was eighty-two years old.

People speak of Jane Long as "the Mother of Texas." It is true that she had the first American child born in Texas, as far as it is known. But that is not the whole reason she is called this. To many people she was their ideal of a good mother. She was kind, brave, able to face hard times, and wise. She was a woman who, when she gave a promise, lived up to her word.

## *The Austins – Father and Son*

When a person wants something, there may be many ways to get it or have it given to him. He may take it or he may work for it. Some ways are better than others.

When Texas was owned by Spain, many Americans wanted to live in Texas. Dr. James Long tried to take Texas by force and he failed. Other men tried another way and succeeded. This is the story of the father and son who opened the way for settlers to come to Texas.

Moses Austin was born in Connecticut. As a young man he ran a store, first in Philadelphia and then in Richmond, Virginia. He had three children and, like a good father, he wanted the best for them. He thought he could make more money if he went into mining. He bought a lead mine in Virginia and then bought a bigger one in Missouri. Missouri was owned then by Spain, so Moses became a Spanish subject. Later Missouri became part of the United States.

Moses made a lot of money which he put into a bank in St. Louis. All went well until the bank failed. Moses lost everything he owned. What could he do? He talked it over with Stephen, his oldest son. Moses decided to go to Texas to try once more to make his fortune. Stephen lent his father fifty dollars to make the trip.

Five days before Christmas in 1820 Moses rode into San Antonio de Bexar. It had taken him a month to come from Little Rock, Arkansas. He was very tired but he lost no time going to the Governor's Palace. He wanted to ask Governor Martinez to let him bring settlers to Texas.

Governor Martinez would not listen to Moses. Because Dr. Long had tried

to take Texas, Spain did not want any Americans in Texas. Moses tried to tell the Governor that he had been a Spanish subject. The Governor did not believe him. Governor Martinez ordered Moses to leave San Antonio before night!

Moses left the Governor a broken old man. He had nothing. He was hundreds of miles from his home. His dreams of starting all over again were gone. What could he do? He did not know anyone. He could not even rest before he must move on. And where could he go?

As Moses crossed the square, a man spoke to him. Moses could not believe his eyes. It was his old friend, Baron de Bastrop. Moses told his friend why he was there and what had happened. The Baron knew the Governor well. He promised to go to the Governor with Moses and this time things were different. Moses told the Governor he wanted to bring in three hundred families to farm and make homes in Texas. They would obey the Spanish laws just as he had in Missouri. They would not fight nor make trouble trading with the Indians. Spain had given land to men who brought settlers to Louisiana. She should do the same for Texas. The Governor listened. It was a good plan. The Governor agreed to give Moses 200,000 acres of land. He felt sure the rulers in Mexico would agree also.

In a few days Moses started back to Missouri. It was a long, hard trip and the weather was very cold and wet. Moses became sick on the way and it took him three months to get home. He hoped to go back to Texas in May, but he was too ill. On June 10, 1820, Moses Austin died.

Stephen Austin was in Natchitoches

when he learned of his father's death. He had come there to go with Moses into Texas, but he did not plan to stay. Stephen was studying law in New Orleans and he hoped to make his home there.

Governor Martinez had sent men to Natchitoches to meet Moses and bring him to San Antonio. Before Moses died, he had told his wife he wanted Stephen to carry out his plans. Stephen had to make up his mind what to do. Should he take his father's place? If he went to Texas, he would have to forget about becoming a lawyer. But if he went back to New Orleans, his father's dream would die. Stephen chose Texas.

There were two reasons for having parties when Stephen came to San Antonio. The people liked the quiet young man. They were glad he had come to take his father's place. That same day word came that Mexico no longer belonged to Spain. It seemed a good beginning for carrying out big plans. But there were troubles ahead for Stephen and Mexico.

Stephen's first job was choosing the land he wanted for his settlers. He took his father's tomahawk and started to explore. He had come through the forests of East Texas where mighty trees stood tall and straight. He passed over rolling hills where grass grew as high as his stirrups. He crossed cool green rivers where he could see fish swimming in the water. Parts of the land were bare and dry, but Stephen loved it all.

Stephen chose a block of land that was almost square. It ran from the Camino Real to the Gulf of Mexico and lay between the Lavaca and the San Jacinto Rivers. The land was beautiful and rich for farming. The streams and rivers gave

people a way to travel even without roads. It was a land to be proud of and Austin wanted very much to tell people about it.

Governor Martinez and Stephen worked out a plan. The head of each family would get 640 acres of land. He might also buy 320 acres for his wife and 160 acres for each of his children. If he had slaves, he could buy 80 acres for each one. And what do you think was the price for the land? Only 12½ cents an acre for surveying and recording the deed! Better still, settlers had to pay only half of this when they came. Stephen would even take cattle or help from the settlers if they did not have the money. But there were two things every settler had to do. He must promise to obey the laws of Mexico and to become a member of the Catholic Church.

Stephen could hardly wait to tell people about his plan. People he spoke to could not believe how cheap the land was. Stephen went to New Orleans to get the story in the papers. As the news spread, people everywhere started thinking about going to Texas.

Stephen bought a ship called The Lively. He loaded it with supplies and it carried about twenty settlers. Stephen told the captain to land at the mouth of the Colorado River. Austin set out by land to meet the ship. He wanted to be there to help the settlers choose the land for their new homes.

The Lively had a safe trip to Texas, but it landed at the wrong place – the mouth of the Brazos River! The captain put the settlers on land and went back to New Orleans. He picked up supplies and settlers and started back to Texas. This time the ship was caught by a bad storm.

It wrecked on Galveston Island. The crew and settlers were picked up by another ship. They, too, were taken to the mouth of the Brazos River. They found the first settlers still there, but none of them could find Austin. He was looking for them at the mouth of the Colorado River! Most of those settlers went back to the United States, but others who came by land stayed. About 150 men were making ready for their families to come. Eight families were already on the land.

When Stephen went to tell Governor Martinez all that had happened, the Governor had bad news for him. The leaders in Mexico did not like Stephen's plan. They would not agree to it. Had Stephen brought people to Texas only to make them go back? Stephen decided that he must go to Mexico City at once to talk to the leaders. He hoped to be gone a short time, but he was there for almost a year. This was when the leaders in Mexico were changing very quickly. If Stephen had not gone, he would not have been

able to bring more settlers in. He left Mexico with more land for each settler and more work for himself. He was now an empresario and a colonel in the army. An empresario was a person who had the right to bring in settlers. He had to see that everyone obeyed Mexican laws and even fight for them if needed.

When Stephen got back to Texas, he found the settlers were unhappy. They had not received needed tools and supplies. The crops had failed because there was little rain. Indians had attacked and stolen food and animals. The settlers did not have titles to their land to show they owned it. Some did not want to pay Austin for getting the titles. They did not understand why Austin had been gone so long.

Stephen and his father's friend, Baron de Bastrop, started to work at once. The Baron made surveys and gave people land titles. Stephen drove the Indians away. He helped plant new crops. New settlers came and everything was better.

Stephen even built a capital for his grant on the banks of the Brazos River. He called it San Felipe de Austin.

Stephen wrote laws for his settlers. Each town had an alcalde or mayor and an ayuntamiento or council. Every town also chose men to lead others in fighting the Indians. They were all under Stephen as the colonel. He was also the chief judge and leader.

Stephen never knew on any day what kinds of problems he might have. It might be helping a settler choose his land. It might be leading soldiers against the Indians. It might be deciding what to do with someone who had broken the law. He only knew he would be busy from sunup until late at night.

By March, 1825, Austin had settled 297 families on his land grant. They are called the "Old Three Hundred." Because he had done such a good job, the leaders of Mexico let Stephen bring in 500 more families. As the years passed Stephen brought in six thousand people to Texas.

There were other empresarios in Texas. Martin de Leon brought in Mexican families and started the town of Victoria. Green De Witt was given a land grant west of Austin's. Gonzales became its capital. Irish settlers went to South Texas on lands of McGloin and McMillan or Power and Heweston. David Burnet, Lorenzo de Zavala, Haden Edwards, Joseph Vehlein, and Benjamin Milam are some other empresarios who got land grants.

As more and more people came to Texas, there were problems. Mexico passed a law saying the settlers could not bring slaves into Texas. She also ruled that Texans would have to pay tax on anything brought into the state. The Texans would not obey these new laws. Then Mexico said no more people from the United States could come to Texas. Mexico thought the Texans wanted to be free but this was not true. The Texans only wanted to become a separate state with their own leaders and laws.

In 1832 the leaders of Texas had a meeting at San Felipe de Austin. They wrote a paper telling just what the people wanted and why. The paper never got to Mexico so the next year there was another meeting. This time they also drew up a constitution for the state they wanted. Someone had to take these papers to Mexico City. They chose Austin for this important job. They looked to him as their wisest leader.

It took Austin three months to get to Mexico City. He found it very different from the last time, but he started to work at once. President Santa Anna was planning to become the dictator of Mexico. He had no time to listen to Austin. Austin wrote to his friends about how things were in Mexico. He asked them to be ready to set up their state government very quickly. At last on December 10, 1833, Austin had good news. The bad law had been set aside and soon Texas might become a separate Mexican state. He started home a happy man.

When Austin arrived in Saltillo on January 3, 1834, he was arrested. The letter he had written had been read. It made some Mexican leaders angry. Stephen was sent back to Mexico City and kept in one jail after another. He was not told why he was in jail nor was he brought to trial. For a while he could not even talk to anyone. At last in October friends

from Texas came to help him. He got out on Christmas Day but it was seven more months before he could go home.

While Austin was in Mexico, things had been happening in Texas. Word had come that Santa Anna was sending troops to Anahuac to help take over Texas. William B. Travis and a group of men took the soldiers at Anahuac instead and sent them to San Antonio. For this, the Mexicans wanted Travis and the others arrested. The Texans would not do that. Some Texans wanted to get ready for war at once. Others wanted to make peace with Santa Anna. They all wanted to know what Austin thought they should do.

Stephen had always been a man of peace. He had tried to make peace with the Indians. He had tried to work with the settlers and the leaders in Mexico. This time was different. Santa Anna had made himself a dictator and wanted

everyone to obey him. Austin knew that Texans would have to stand up for their rights and be ready to fight. He asked the people to choose their wisest men to decide what they should do.

Before the leaders could meet, there was a fight over a cannon. The town of Gonzales had been given a cannon to use against the Indians. When Mexican soldiers tried to take it, the Texans fired on the enemy. At once, men from all over Texas started for Gonzales. Austin went, too, because the men made him leader of the army.

It was a strange army. There were no uniforms nor supplies. Every man walked or rode his own horse or mule. Each man used his own gun and gun powder and brought what food he had. Everyone was used to looking after himself. They did not know how to take orders, but Austin was able to get them to work together.

Most of the Mexican soldiers in Texas were in San Antonio. Austin and about 300 men marched to San Antonio. As they went others joined them. Two groups of Mexican settlers came, one from Victoria, another from near San Antonio. They brought word that the people of San Antonio would help in any way they could.

Austin wanted to attack at once. Many wanted to wait until the leaders set up a government. The government was needed to secure guns and supplies for the army and deal with Mexico. Someone had to go to the United States to get help. The leaders asked Austin to go and he left at once. Without help, the Texans could not win.

Austin made many friends for Texas. He got money and other things that were needed. He wanted to get the United States to let Texas become a state, but this he could not do. He did not get back to Texas until after the Battle of San Jacinto.

Ever since he had come to Texas, Austin had worked for the people he had brought here. Now he hoped to do things for himself – to live his dream. He wanted to have his own family and to farm. He wanted to read and visit with friends. He wanted to be a Texan just like everybody else, but this was not to be. The people of Texas turned to him as their leader. They asked him to run for president of the Republic of Texas. He really did not want to run, but he did.

Sam Houston, the hero of the Battle of San Jacinto, also ran for president. He was a big, fine-looking man and people were proud of him. He won the election and became the first president of the Republic of Texas.

Houston asked Austin to be his Secretary of State. It was as hard a job as being president. Stephen had dealt with leaders in the United States and Mexico. He had much experience in government. Once more Austin put the good of the people before his own wishes. He agreed to do it.

Austin worked night and day on hundreds of things needed by the new government. He put his mind and heart into what he was doing and did not think of his body. As he pushed himself to do more and more, he became very tired. Just before Christmas in 1836 Stephen took a very bad cold. Every day he grew worse. On December 27, 1836, Stephen Fuller Austin died. He was forty-three years old.

When President Houston learned of Austin's death, he told the people that "the Father of Texas is no more." Everyone was very sad. They felt lost without Austin. There were other leaders, but they looked first to Stephen. He had opened the way for them to live in Texas. He had helped them choose their land and get started. He had dealt with their problems and given them good advice. He was the one they had turned to when no one else knew what or how to do something. But most of all, he wanted the best for everyone in Texas. He was truly the "Father of Texas."

## *The Seguins – Father and Son*

When a person moves to a place that is strange to him, whether he likes it or not may depend upon whether he finds friends. When Moses Austin first came to Texas, he found an old friend, Baron de Bastrop, who helped him get a land grant. When Stephen Austin came, he found many new friends – Mexican leaders who welcomed him and helped him in many ways.

Erasmo Seguin (ā-räś-mō sā-gēń) was one of the first of Austin's new friends. He and several other men had been sent to Natchitoches, Louisiana, to meet Moses, but instead they found Stephen. They were sad to learn that Moses was dead and they wondered if Stephen could carry out his father's duties as empresario. Erasmo thought Stephen should have the chance to prove himself and he promised to help Stephen. With every mile they traveled together toward San Antonio, Erasmo felt more sure of Stephen. They became true friends for all of their lives.

Austin learned many interesting things about his new friend. Erasmo had been born in San Fernando de Bexar, or San Antonio, in 1782. He was very smart and was one of the first persons in Texas to raise cotton on his ranch near Floresville. That ranch became a welcome stopping place for travelers to Texas, as did the Seguin home in San Antonio.

Erasmo had been one of the leaders who set up a school for all the children in San Antonio as early as 1812. He knew how important learning was and in many matters that were for the good of people in the town, he led the way. That is why he was the first alcalde in San Antonio in 1820.

When the men reached San Antonio, they learned that Mexico no longer belonged to Spain. The people of Mexico had been trying to gain freedom for many years and the Mexicans in San Antonio were happy this had happened. Now Mexico had to decide how to govern itself since all the old rules had been taken away.

In 1823 Erasmo Seguin was chosen to go to Mexico City for Texas to help start the new government and to pass new laws. Because Erasmo was a friend of the settlers and he understood their needs, he was able to have laws passed that were good for them. There was one thing he could not do. He was unable to have Texas made a separate state because there were not enough people living in Texas. Texas and Coahuila became one state with the seat of the government in Coahuila.

During the next ten years, Erasmo and many other Mexicans stood with the settlers in their demands from the Mexican government. He believed Mexico should set up good schools for all the children in Texas. He thought the settlers should have the right to have slaves to work the fields. Most of all, he felt that Texas should be a separate state.

In 1833 the people of Texas got together in a convention. The leaders wrote a paper telling why Texas should now be a separate state and they drew up a constitution to show how it would govern itself. Stephen Austin, Dr. James Miller, and Erasmo Seguin were asked to take the papers to Mexico and give them to the government. Since Erasmo was so highly thought of both in Mexico and Texas, the leaders felt sure he could get the Mexican leaders to listen. As it happened, neither Seguin nor Dr. Miller were able to make the trip, so Austin went alone.

Juan Seguin was Erasmo's oldest son and, like his father, was a good friend of Austin and the settlers. He also was a leader in San Antonio and was the alcalde in 1834 when there was trouble with the government of the state of Coahuila-Texas. The governor and other state leaders disagreed where the capital should be. Some wanted it in Saltillo and others wanted it in Monclova. Neither side would give in, so they set up two governments.

Juan and Erasmo called for persons in Texas to meet to set up its own government until the matter could be settled in Coahuila. Austin was still in Mexico and perhaps they thought this would prove that Texas could govern itself wisely, but the people of Texas would not come. Austin was in jail and many were afraid that such an act would cause him to be killed by the Mexicans.

At that same time Santa Anna had just set himself up as dictator. He made his brother-in-law, General Cos, the commander of the Eastern Provinces, or states, of Mexico. General Cos first did away with the government of the state of Coahuila-Texas and then he sent Colonel Ugartechea with many soldiers to Texas. General Cos planned to come to Texas later himself. The people of Texas did not want to be under the rule of the army, but the people were of two minds. Some wanted to fight the Mexican soldiers at once, but others hoped to be able to make peace with Santa Anna.

Although nothing had come of Juan and Erasmo's plans to set up a govern-

ment in Texas, General Cos spoke out strongly against the Seguins. This did not frighten either man. Juan started getting Mexicans from the ranches along the San Antonio River ready to fight for Texas if war should break out against Mexico. Erasmo, too, started thinking how best he could help.

When General Cos reached San Antonio, he made Erasmo give up his job as postmaster. General Cos also made Erasmo walk the thirty-three miles to his ranch at Floresville. While Erasmo walked, he decided what he could do to help Texas. He would make his ranch a storehouse for all the things the Texans would need when the time came to fight.

When Austin got back to Texas in September, 1835, he knew that Texas would have to fight for her freedom. He had always tried to keep the peace, but now this was not possible. Men from all over Texas started for San Antonio to fight General Cos. Erasmo and his San Antonio neighbor, Jim Bowie, joined the army. Juan lead all the Mexican ranchers to the Texas camp and he was even able to get some of Cos' soldiers to leave the Mexican army and fight for the Texans. Juan was with Jim Bowie at the Battle of Concepcion while Erasmo helped get many supplies for the army. No one was happier than the Seguins when at last General Cos raised a white flag and gave up his arms. Juan and William Travis followed the Mexican army to see that it left Texas and on their return they brought back many horses for the Texas cavalry.

Many people thought the war was over and went back to their farms and ranches. Erasmo could see more trouble ahead so

he put up great stores of food, blankets, horses, and livestock. He gave these to Colonel James Fannin and others who were fighting near Goliad and Refugio while he continued to add to his supplies. Juan was made a captain in the cavalry in January, 1836, and he was given orders to report to Colonel William Travis at the Alamo. Travis knew Juan well and he knew Sequin could get through the enemy's lines if anyone could. Juan was far from the Alamo trying to get help when the brave men there met death. As soon as he heard the news, Sequin rode toward Gonzales as fast as he could to join General Houston.

Both of the Seguins, father and son, did all that they could to help the cause of freedom. When the women and children of Texas were running from the enemy toward the east, Juan was in charge of the rear guard of the army. He saw to it that no families were left behind and he and his men helped the people along the muddy roads and across the flooding rivers and streams. Erasmo knew the people needed supplies as much as the army. He drove three thousand sheep behind the families to give them food and help on the way.

Juan and Mosely Baker and the men under their command were sent by

General Houston to San Felipe with orders to keep Santa Anna from crossing the Brazos River. The Brazos was flooded from the spring rains and it was very dangerous to cross. Seguin and Baker burned the town and crossed the river to the east side, taking all the boats of the town with them. When Santa Anna and his soldiers reached the Brazos, they had no way to get to the other side. Santa Anna sent soldiers along the river to try to find boats but there were none, so the Mexican army moved down stream to Thompson's Ferry near Fort Bend. By slowing Santa Anna down, Juan Seguin and Mosely Baker gave General Houston much needed time to train his army for the battle yet to come.

Seguin and his men joined General Houston in time to fight bravely in the Battle of San Jacinto. Once more Seguin, this time with Henry Karnes, followed the Mexican army as it left Texas. Juan saw to it that the enemy did not take nor destroy things that belonged to the Texans.

In May, 1836, Juan Seguin was made lieutenant colonel and told to run the government of San Antonio until the regular government could take over. Many of the Mexicans in San Antonio were afraid because people from the United States who had come to help fight saw all Mexicans as enemies. They did not know that without the help of people like the Seguins and many other Mexicans, the war might have been lost. Erasmo and Juan worked hard to bring about good feelings and understanding between the Mexicans and the Anglos. One job was especially hard for Juan. He buried the ashes of the heroes of the Alamo, many of whom had been his true friends.

The government of Mexico did not accept the treaty Santa Anna signed with Texas and at times they sent soldiers to take Texas back. In 1837 when General Felix Huston was the head of the Texas army, he ordered Juan Seguin to destroy San Antonio. The General felt that the two could not be defended from attack and he wanted Seguin to move all the people to the Brazos River. Seguin could not see his town destroyed and he asked President Houston to change this order. The President did so, but Seguin made an enemy of General Felix Huston who made it very hard for Seguin.

In 1838 Juan Seguin left the army and became a senator in the Texas Congress. He tried to bring about good feelings between the Mexicans and the Anglos. He also asked that laws be printed in both English and in Spanish so that all the people could read them. He wanted Texas to be a country where everyone was a Texan first and a Mexican or Anglo second.

During the time between the meetings of the senate, Juan joined John C. Hayes in fights against the Comanches. Hays was one of the leaders of the Texas Rangers and Seguin was a welcome member of that special group of brave men. People liked Juan so much that the town of Walnut Spring changed it name to Seguin in his honor.

In January, 1841, Juan was made the mayor of San Antonio. It was a town that had changed much since 1834 when Juan was the alcalde. Many of the Anglo settlers were new to Texas and they knew nothing of the early leaders and the events that had happened while Texas was part of Mexico. They looked on Mex-icans as all being alike and they did not trust them. Someone spread the story that Seguin had told the Mexican leaders about the Santa Fe Expedition and had caused all its members to be put in jail. This was a lie, but some people who did not know Juan believed it. Others only remembered it, but in spite of this, Juan was elected mayor again in 1842.

The Mexican government thought it must do something in return for the Santa Fe Expedition. It sent word that Texas must return to Mexico as a state at once or it would suffer. Through a letter from a man in Mexico named Rafael Vasquez, Seguin learned that the Mexi-cans were planning to capture San Antonio and he was told to leave town. Stories like this were spread around quite often. In March Seguin was at his ranch on business when, true enough, Vasquez did take San Antonio. The Mex-ican soldiers stayed only two days, but Vasquez told people that Seguin was his friend. For many new settlers this showed that Seguin could not be trusted.

When Seguin returned from his ranch, the people of the town were very angry with him. General Burleson had to go to San Antonio to keep the peace, but Burleson trusted Seguin and was sorry for his friend. Seguin was very hurt that the people did not trust him and in April he left his office as mayor and went to Mexico.

It is true that Seguin had friends in Mexico, but he also had an enemy – a very important one. Santa Anna knew how much Juan and his father Erasmo had done to help Texas become free from Mexico. When he found out that Juan was in Mexico, Santa Anna gave him a choice. Seguin could either go to prison for the rest of his life or serve in the Mexican army. Juan took the service in the army as the better of the two. Santa Anna put Juan in the army under General Adrian Woll.

On September 11, 1842, General Woll and fourteen hundred Mexican soldiers reached San Antonio and captured the town. The Mexicans took fifty-three men who were there in court and started marching them back to Mexico. When this news spread, Texans went to San Antonio and started after the Mexican army. There was a battle at Salado Creek that lasted all day, but during the night General Woll drew his soldiers back and started again for Mexico.

Juan Seguin had been seen wearing the uniform of the Mexicans and fighting many men he had known as friends. For many people this was the last time they ever wanted to see or hear of Juan. They remembered the lie about his part in the Santa Fe Expedition. They remembered that Rafael Vasquez had called Seguin his friend when he captured San Antonio. And now here was Juan Seguin fighting against the Texans as a Mexican. They never once thought about all he had done for Texas.

Juan Seguin went back to Mexico. In 1845 he wrote to President Anson Jones asking that Texas not join the United States. He said that he felt Mexico would agree at last to peace with Texas and to her independence. However, the Congress of the Republic of Texas had already decided to join the United States. Peace with Mexico had to wait for two more years when the Treaty of Guadalupe-Hidalgo was signed by Mexico and the United States.

In 1848 Juan Seguin asked to be able to return to Texas and he was allowed to come home. Erasmo, his father, was still living at his ranch and it must have been a time of gladness and sadness for both. It was good to be together and, when they thought of the early days in Texas, they had many good memories of friends like Austin and others. The last few years were times of sadness for both father and son.

In 1857 Erasmo died. He was honored by both Mexican and Anglo friends. Juan lived thirty-two years longer and he died in Nuevo Laredo. Both men did much for Texas. They shared their country, their money, and their friendship with those who came to Texas. They were Mexican and were proud of it, but there was one thing they valued most of all. They were Texans, tried and true, and for them, that was the best anyone could be!

## Benjamin Milam – The First Texas Hero

Some people are afraid to take chances. Others like the excitement of trying new things. Ben Milam took chances all of his life. Sometimes what happened was good and at other times bad. But no matter what happened, people liked Ben and counted on him.

Milam first came to Texas in 1818 when he was thirty years old. He came to trade with the Comanche Indians living along the Colorado River. Most people feared the Comanches, but Ben wrote that they were kind and gentle. He found them taking care of David Burnet while he was sick. Perhaps Ben understood Indians better than most people. He had grown up in Kentucky where Indians from the north and south hunted.

Ben learned that Mexico was fighting to be free from Spain. Texas was part of the Mexican state of Coahuila. Ben saw what a beautiful place Texas was and he thought it was worth fighting for. He went to New Orleans to join up and was made a colonel by General Trespalacios. Dr. James Long and the General were planning to go to Bolivar. Ben went on the ship that took Jane Long and others who had come to fight. Dr. Long asked Milam to look after his wife and child until he arrived.

General Trespalacios, Dr. Long, and Ben made plans to capture Texas. Dr. Long was to capture Goliad and then march south. Ben and General Trespalacios were to raise an army and meet Dr. Long and his men in Mexico. This seemed like a good plan but it did not work. Instead Dr. Long

was taken prisoner and so were Ben and the General. All three men were sent to Mexico City.

Ben and Dr. Long became best friends, but the General and Dr. Long had a falling out. Dr. Long asked Ben to be a brother to his wife and a father to his children if anything should happen to him. Perhaps the doctor had a feeling about what would happen, for the next day Dr. Long was killed. Ben thought the General had planned the doctor's death. He tried to find out, but Ben was put in jail himself.

When Ben got out of Mexico, he went to find Jane. He had kept all of Dr. Long's papers and other things. True to his promise Ben tried to take care of Jane all of his life.

In 1824 Ben went to Mexico again. This time he wanted to get a grant of land to bring settlers into Texas. General Trespalacios wrote a letter saying that Milam had fought to free Mexico from Spain. This gave him the right to money and land in Texas. Milam became a Mexican citizen, but it was two years before he got a grant of eleven leagues. He had six years in which to settle 300 families on it.

What did Milam do while he was waiting for his grant? He must have looked for mines, for he had many. He also made friends with people like Jim Bowie and General Arthur Wavell. The General asked Ben to be his land agent for his grant along the Red River. Milam agreed and settled at Lake Comfort, but this place brought him little comfort.

Colin McKinney, a neighbor of

Ben's, had a beautiful daughter named Annie. Ben fell in love with her and she promised to marry him. Ben had to go to Mexico City to see General Wavell, but he hoped to be back soon. The General sent Milam to England to deal with some bankers who wanted to buy land and mines in Texas. Ben left in June, 1828, and was gone for more than a year. He thought about Annie and bought beautiful silver and furniture for their home. He could hardly wait to see Annie, but how sad was their meeting. Annie had not heard from Ben during all the long months and she had married someone else! Ben left Texas and went north.

In Cincinnati, Ben met David Burnet again, the man the Comanches had nursed back to health. Ben and David decided to form a company to work Milam's silver mines. They also wanted to bring people to live on their land grants. They hired men to sell stock in their "Western Colonization and Mining Company." The men they hired sold stock, but they did not tell the buyers the truth. When the buyers learned that the sellers were lying, they took their money back.

Almost five years had passed since Ben had received his land grant. He had been so busy with other things he had not done anything about his own grant. He worked very hard and by the end of the next year he had fifty-two families living there. Because he had brought in fewer than 300 settlers, the Mexican leaders would not give him more time. Poor

Ben. Another disappointment!

The settlers along the Red River had never received titles to their lands. They asked Ben to go to Mexico for them. On his way he stopped by Brazoria where many of the leaders in Texas lived. Ben had a plan that would help all settlers who had no title to their land. He wanted the Governor of the state to choose seven men to settle all land claims. The seven men to be called "commissioners" would be paid $5.00 for every title. The Texas leaders thought this was a very good plan. They wrote a letter to the Governor asking that the plan be set up.

Brazoria was also the place where Jane Long had her boarding house. Ben wanted to see how she was getting along. She was as brave and beautiful as ever. It had been years since Dr. Long had been killed but Jane had never married. Whether she promised to marry Ben is not known for sure. Many people thought they became engaged.

Milam went to Monclova where the state legislature was meeting. The Governor and the legislators listened and agreed to Ben's plan. They also made him the Commissioner for the people along the Red River. Everything was fine until word came that General Cos was on the way. General Cos had orders from Santa Anna to take over the government.

The Governor, some of the legislators, and Milam started for Texas at once. They had not gone far before they were captured and taken back to Monterrey, Mexico. Since Ben was not part of the government, he was treated better than the others. The people who were holding him let him go to the creek every day to take a bath. One day Ben found a horse with supplies waiting for him near the creek. Ben did not stop to thank his friend nor to take a bath. He jumped on the horse and headed for Texas as fast as he could go.

It is a long way from Monterrey to where Ben wanted to go. He had to watch out for Mexican soldiers and unfriendly Indians. He kept away from the trails where he might find people who would take him back to Mexico. Many times he was not quite sure where he was.

One night while he was resting under some small trees, he heard voices. He listened carefully. Were they Mexican soldiers speaking Spanish? At first he could not tell. Then he was sure. They were Texans. Without a sound he drew closer until he could see the men. Then he called and showed himself to them. The men could hardly believe their eyes. They had thought Ben was dead, but how glad they were to see him.

The Texans were on their way to Goliad to take the fort from Mexican soldiers. Ben was happy to join them and that same night they attacked. After they shot the guard, they broke into the room of the commander. The Mexicans gave up at once and the next day Ben took the three officers to Gonzales. He then hurried to San Antonio.

Men from all over Texas had made camp near San Antonio. They were waiting for others to come before attacking the city. Stephen Austin was the leader of this Texas army. Austin was glad to see Ben, for he wanted him to lead a company of scouts. The scouts were to take any Mexican soldiers they might find. They also were to choose the best place for the Texans to cross the San Antonio River.

When Ben got back to San Antonio, he, Jim Bowie, and William Travis were sent toward the Rio Grande River. They were to find out about any other Mexican soldiers on the way to Texas. Ben came back to San Antonio seven weeks later. He found that things had changed a great deal while he had been gone. Stephen Austin was no longer the leader of the army. He was in the United States trying to raise money and supplies for Texas. Burleson was now the commander of the army. He and the officers had decided to camp outside of San Antonio for the winter. Yet, Ben learned, General Cos and his men were in San Antonio. Ben thought it was time to fight. If others were afraid to lead, Ben was not.

"Who will go with old Ben Milam into San Antonio?" Milam called.

At once men began to gather around Ben. In no time there were three hundred or more men. It must have pleased Milam to find so many ready to follow him. Ben thanked the men and set about making his plans. He chose to go into town from two sides and use two houses as headquarters.

Ben and his men put the plan

into action on December 5, 1835.
General Cos also had two places for
his soldiers. One was in the square of
the town and the other was in the
Alamo. The fighting was heavy with
each side firing at the other. Ben and
his men used the de la Garza house
for their headquarters. Colonel
Johnson and his men were in the
Veramendi house.

On December 7, Ben Milam left
the de la Garza house. Perhaps he
needed to talk to the other Texans.
Perhaps he wanted to help someone

who was wounded. He ran quickly.
Just as he reached the courtyard of
the Veramendi house it happened.
A bullet from a Mexican gun caught
him. Ben Milam fell to the
ground dead.

All firing stopped. The Texans
could not believe what had happened.
Then it was as though every man
had the same thought at the very
same time. The Texans were not
fighting just for themselves. They
were fighting for Ben Milam.

From that moment on, the Texans
fought harder than ever before. They
fought from house to house, up one
street and down another. No place
was safe from them.

On the morning of December 9, a
white flag flew over the Alamo. Were
the Mexicans ready to give up? The
Texans still kept their guns ready.
The next day the Texans had the
answer. General Cos signed a paper
giving up all the supplies and money
of this Mexican army. He also promised to take his soldiers out of Texas.

It was a day of mixed feelings for
the Texans. They were glad they had
won, but sad that they had lost Ben,
their brave leader. They were proud
of themselves, too. They had been
ready when their hero called "Who
will go with old Ben Milam into San
Antonio?" They hoped that this would
be the end of fighting and that they
could go home, but it was just the
beginning. There would be many
other heroes, but none braver than
the first hero of the Texas Revolution
– Ben Milam.

## *The Alamo*

Where did you get your name? Were you named for someone in your family or was it chosen for its meaning? Some people think that a child's name will have much to do with what he becomes. Perhaps that is the reason kings have been named Richard. That name means "powerful king." Other names show how people feel about their children. Sara means "princess" and Beatrice means "happiness."

Places get their names in different ways, too. The city of Austin was named for Stephen F. Austin, and El Paso was the pass to the north from Mexico. The mission called the Alamo had three other names first. In Mexico it was called San Francisco Solano. When it was moved to Texas, it was named San Antonio de Padua. Next it was known as San Antonio de Valero. But when the mission was closed, it became the Alamo.

No one knows just why the name was chosen. The word Alamo means "cottonwood tree" in Spanish. Perhaps it was because many cottonwoods grew around the old mission. Perhaps it was because of the Mexican soldiers who lived within its walls at times. The soldiers came from a village called San Jose y Santiago del Alamo de Parras. Whatever the reason for its name, the Alamo has a very special meaning for every Texan.

From its closing in 1794 until 1835, the Alamo was used very little. There was no one to keep up the buildings so they showed signs of the weather. Sometimes soldiers would stay there, but never for very long. For a while it was a hospital for soldiers and for the people who lived in San Antonio. It was a prison for three months in 1813, but the Alamo is not

remembered for any of these reasons. It is remembered because of the brave men who gave their lives there so that Texas could be free. How did all of this happen?

When Stephen Austin and other empresarios brought people to Texas, the settlers promised to obey the Mexican laws. All went well for several years, but Mexico was having its troubles. The leaders changed very often and so did their ideas about Texas. New laws were passed that would not let any more Americans come to Texas. The people also had to pay taxes on everything that was brought into Texas. They could not have slaves to help them work the land. Texans asked that the laws be changed but instead tax collectors were sent. There were several fights between the Mexican soldiers and the Texans. This made the Mexican leaders angry. They asked that the Texas leaders be turned over to the Mexican soldiers. The Texans refused.

Santa Anna became the president of Mexico. He promised to obey the Mexican constitution but he really wanted to be a dictator. He sent soldiers to break up the state governments. He sent his brother-in-law, General Cos to Monclova. That is where the Coahuila-Texas legislature was meeting. Then General Cos was ordered to go to Texas where he was to take the Texas leaders and punish them.

When word reached Texas that General Cos was on the way, Texans started for Gonzales. The men chose Stephen Austin for their leader. Soon there was an army of three hundred men. More joined on the march to San Antonio. General Cos was already there with hundreds of trained

Mexican soldiers.

The Texans made camp outside the city. The Mexicans could not get out, nor could more Mexican soldiers and supplies get in. The Mexicans became worried. It was the right time for the Texans to attack and on December 5, the fighting began.

The battle lasted four days and nights. The Texans drove the Mexicans from the plaza in the town to the Alamo. On December 9, 1835, a white flag flew over the Alamo. General Cos gave up! He left all his supplies and promised to leave Texas and never come back. By Christmas there was not a Mexican soldier in Texas. What a good Christmas present! Many settlers thought the war was over, but this was far from the end.

When Santa Anna learned what General Cos had done, he was white with anger. He gathered his soldiers from all over Mexico and got ready to march. He would teach the Texans who their ruler was! He would make them pay!

The Texas army had broken up after the battle. Many men went home to their families. Some wanted to take the fight to Matamoros, Mexico. Colonel Fannin sent out a call for soldiers to march to Goliad with him. Colonel Johnson, who had been in command at the Alamo, wanted to go, too. He took all but one hundred and four soldiers with all the clothes, supplies, and money from the Alamo. He left Colonel Neill in charge. All of this was done without orders from General Sam Houston!

General Houston ordered Jim Bowie to go to the Alamo with about twenty-five men. They were to take the cannons in the Alamo to Gonzales and blow up the mission. Houston knew that the Alamo could not be defended against Santa Anna's army. Sad to say, his orders were not carried out. Colonel Neill did not have teams of horses to pull the cannons. He and Jim Bowie decided to strengthen the old mission and ask the Texas leaders for men, clothes, and supplies.

The Texas leaders asked William B. Travis to get one hundred men to go to the Alamo. Travis tried very hard but he got only about one third of that number. Travis and his men reached the Alamo on February 3. A few days later Colonel Neill was called home because of sickness. This left two men in charge – Jim Bowie and William Travis. Both wanted to be the commander. Most of the men wanted Bowie, but Travis had the higher rank. So it ended that Travis commanded the regular soldiers and Bowie the rest.

The Alamo had high walls but it was not ready for battle. Everyone knew that Santa Anna would arrive soon. The Texans used the days before the Mexican army came to make ready. Under Jim Bowie's orders they piled dirt around the walls and built wood walkways on top. They put cannons at the places where they could fire best at the enemy. They got food and as many supplies as they could find. Jim was everywhere, but one day he fell from the high wall. He hurt his hip very badly and from then on gave commands from his bed.

What the Alamo needed most was men. Travis wrote letters to the Texas leaders asking for soldiers. He sent James Bonham to Colonel Fannin begging him to come to the Alamo with his four hundred soldiers. He wrote to the people of Gonzales where the army was gathering. He asked them to come at once to the Alamo. Surely it was only a matter of time until help would come.

On February 19, Davy Crockett and about a dozen of his "boys" arrived at the Alamo. The Texans and the people of San Antonio had a big party for them. Davy played his fiddle and everyone danced and had a good time. On February 22, there was another party. This was in honor of George Washington's birthday. The Texans felt that their revolution was being fought for freedom just as had the American Revolution. That same night word came that Santa Anna was only about twenty miles away.

On February 23, Santa Anna and about 3000 soldiers took over the town of San Antonio. He sent word to Jim Bowie to give up at once with no conditions. By this time Bowie was ill with high fever. He thought they should at least talk with the General, but Travis did not. He answered with a cannon shot in the air. Santa Anna replied by lifting a blood red flag over the San Fernando Church. This ment there was to be a fight to the death!

For the next eleven days Santa Anna's soldiers shelled the Alamo night and day. The Mexican army was getting larger all the time. Its soldiers could take turns resting, but the Texans had to be on guard every minute. Davy Crockett and his sharp shooters kept the enemy at a distance, but the Texans did not fire their cannons. They needed to save their shells for the coming battle.

On March 1, Captain Albert Martin and thirty-one men slipped into the Alamo. They had been in Gonzales when the letter from Travis had come. What an act of bravery! Each man knew he would give his life, but he did so to try to save the lives of his family.

On March 3, James Bonham dashed into the Alamo. He was the last man to go into its gates. He had gone to Colonel Fannin to get help, but it was not coming. Fannin had started for the Alamo, but his wagons carrying cannons broke down. He turned back. Everyone at the Alamo knew what that meant. They had no one but themselves to fight an army of almost five thousand men.

Colonel Travis called all the men together. He told them that there was no chance of anyone coming to help them. If anyone wanted to leave, no one would hold that against him. He himself had chosen to stay and hold Santa Anna's army as long as possible. This would give other Texans a chance to get out of Texas, or get ready to fight. Then he drew a line on the dirt floor with his sword. He asked those who wanted to stay with him to step over the line. At once every man but two crossed to Travis' side. Jim Bowie was one. He was lying on a cot so very ill, but he asked that he be carried over. The other man, Moses Rose, stood alone on the other side. That night Rose slipped over the wall.

That same day Travis sent out his last letter to the Texas leaders. John Smith carried it through the Mexican lines to Washington-on-the-Brazos. The Texas leaders had no men to send. Even if they had, the men would have gotten there too late to help. The men at the Alamo never knew that they were fighting for a Texas that had declared its independence from Mexico on March 2!

General Santa Anna and his officers met on March 4. Some wanted to attack at once. Others wanted to wait until March 7 when more cannons would arrive. Santa Anna sent word to his soldiers on March 5 that they would attack before dawn on March 6. That day they were to make ladders to climb the walls of the Alamo. The cavalry would be behind the foot soldiers. This way neither foot soldiers nor Texans could get away. The attack would be from all four sides.

There were 187 men in the Alamo. Nineteen of them were from England and Europe. Thirty-two were from Tennessee. There were nine or ten Mexicans who had lived in Texas all their lives. The rest of the men were from other states in America. Travis told each of them where he should stand during the battle. It was decided that the church would be the last stand of the battle. The few families living in the Alamo with their men were to stay in the church as was Jim Bowie.

If Travis were to fall, Captain Baugh was to take command. Should he also be killed, Davy Crockett was the next to lead. Major Evans was told to be ready to blow up the gunpowder which was in one room in the church. Everyone knew his post.

On March 5, the Mexican guns were quiet. Santa Anna knew the Texans were worn out by the constant shelling. He wanted the Texans to sleep. He hoped to have his soldiers pouring over the Alamo walls before the Texans could get fully awake.

The first sound of attack came from the feet of Mexican soldiers as they ran toward the Alamo. Then there was the sound of the bugle. Most terrible to all was the sound of the Mexican band playing Deguello. This was a battle march meaning "no quarter!"

The Texans sprang to their posts.

Travis dashed to the north wall. It was the only place where the Mexican guns had broken the top of the wall. Davy Crockett and his boys stood behind the stockade between the church and the south wall. James Bonham fired a cannon from the roof of the church. Jim Bowie, so ill he could not hold his head up, lay on his cot with two pistols and his Bowie knife near his hands.

A great wave of Mexican soldiers rushed toward the Alamo. A blast of shells and bullets from the Texans caught the Mexican line and stopped it. The Mexicans had not expected such a blow. They drew back and formed their line again. A second time they rushed forward only to be met with the same deadly fire. Santa Anna was very angry. The Alamo was to be taken at any cost and every Texan was to be killed!

The third attack came with such great force there was no stopping it. This time many more Mexicans rushed to the north wall where it was broken. They set up ladders and climbed over each other to reach the top. Even as the Texans shot the first, others pushed over his body to get inside the Alamo walls. Once inside the fighting became hand to hand, with Mexicans and Texans in deadly combat.

Travis fell by his cannon at the north wall with a bullet in his head. Captain Baugh took over command, but he soon was another victim. The Texans were able to turn one cannon around to fire inside the walls, but there was no stopping Santa Anna's men. They were everywhere in the old mission, going from house to house and room to room looking for Texans.

Davy Crockett and his men stood their ground in front of the church. Someone loaded guns for Davy while he took aim at the never-ending, ever-growing crowd of Mexican soldiers. When there was no more powder nor people to load it, Davy and his men used their guns as clubs. When his body was found it was in the middle of many dead Mexicans.

On top of the church James Bonham kept up firing his cannon. The Mexicans blasted open the door to the church and rushed in only to be shot from above. Yet the Texans could not stand against the hail of bullets. Major Evans, true to his duty, started for the room where the gunpowder was kept. Before he could throw his torch, he fell dead halfway to his post.

The final Mexican prize was Jim Bowie. When the soldiers broke into the room where he lay, they were met by shots from two pistols. Ill as he was, Jim made those two shots count. In a kind of madness, the Mexican soldiers rushed to his cot and stabbed his body again and again.

Suddenly it was over. In just over an hour, every Texan was dead, but so were many Mexicans. For every Texan killed, about eight Mexicans had died. It was a terrible price for both sides. All of the Mexican soldiers were buried, but Santa Anna ordered the bodies of the Texans to be burned.

The only people in the Alamo who were not harmed were Mrs. Almaron Dickinson, her baby, a few Mexican families, and some slaves. Santa Anna wanted Mrs. Dickinson to tell the story of the Alamo. He thought this would bring terror to all Texans. It is true that the story frightened many people. They started running to Lousisiana and safety, but that is not the whole story. Little did Santa Anna know that the memory of the Alamo would play a big part in his own defeat.

Today you can go to the Alamo – the place where 187 brave men died for freedom on March 6, 1836. The rest of the mission is no more, but the church still stands. You can go into the room where the gunpowder was kept. You can see paintings of some of the men who gave their lives there. But more than that you can feel a part of history. You will be walking where Texas heroes, both Anglo and Mexican, lived and died. You will understand why the name of the Alamo has such special meaning to Texans and to all who love freedom.

## Jim Bowie

What kind of man would rope an alligator and ride him? He would have to be strong and know how to handle a rope. He would have to be brave and daring. And especially, he would have to love adventure. That's just the kind of man Jim Bowie was!

As a boy in Louisiana, Jim spent his days hunting, fishing, and exploring the swamps. He learned to throw a knife and hit the target every time. He loved to catch wild horses and ride them. He grew to be over six feet tall and he was good-looking with red curly hair.

When Jim was eighteen, he left home to make his own way. He ran a saw mill and farmed. He made good money and many friends, but the call of adventure was strong. Jim heard that Jean Lafitte, the pirate, was sailing in the Gulf of Mexico. Lafitte was using Galveston Island for his port, so Jim went there to see him. Bowie had heard of riches in Texas and he wanted to find out about them.

Lafitte's riches were from the ships he had taken, but he wanted to sell his prizes. Jim and his brother, Rezin, agreed to buy from Lafitte and do their own trading. Many times this meant selling slaves in New Orleans for one dollar a pound.

Jim next heard that Dr. James Long was going to free Texas from Mexico. He joined others going to Bolivar to set up a fort. By this time Lafitte had left Galveston Island, but Jim and Dr. Long fought Karankawa Indians there. Jim also went with Dr. Long on his march to Goliad. After Dr. Long's death Jim went back to Louisiana.

Jim and Rezin bought land, started

sugar plantations, and built the first steam sugar mill in Louisiana. On one of his hunting trips, Jim cut his finger badly. This would not have happened if there had been a guard between the handle and the blade of his knife. Rezin had just such a knife made from a large, broad file. Jim liked it so much that he had the same blacksmith make knives for his friends. That same knife got Jim into trouble many times. Bowie was a pleasant man, but when he became angry he was ready to fight.

In 1828 Jim came to Texas to live. He had heard many stories about lost gold and silver mines and he wanted to look for them. For three years he found nothing, but he never gave up. He felt sure he would find a silver mine near the San Saba Mission. The Lipan Indians knew where the mines were, but anyone who told would be killed.

Jim lived with the Lipans for several months and found out what he wanted to know. He went back to San Antonio and got Rezin and nine men to go back to the mission with him. On the way back, Jim learned that an Indian war party was looking for him. The Indians struck when Jim and his friends were almost to the mission. There were 164 Indians against eleven white men. The fighting lasted for thirteen hours. Bowie lost one man and three others were wounded, but they killed 82 Indians. Jim and his men got to the mission, but they never found the mine.

In 1830 Jim became a Mexican citizen. The next year he married Maria de Veramendi. She was the beautiful daughter of the vice governor of the state. After a wedding trip to New Orleans, Jim and his bride lived in San Antonio. In Saltillo, Mexico, Jim and his father-in-law set up a cotton mill which Senor Veramendi ran. It was a very happy time for all of them.

In June, 1833, Jim sent his wife and children to the summer home of Senor Veramendi in Monclova. He went to New Orleans on business and hoped to join them soon. It was October before he could leave. Just as he was leaving he got the saddest news of his life. His wife, children, father-in-law – all the Veramendi family – had died of cholera!

After Jim sold the mill in Saltillo, he came back to Texas. He began to sell land, but Stephen Austin did not like the way Jim did business. This did not worry Jim, but it would matter to him later. Jim had many friends, both American and Mexican. He was chosen to go to the state legislature in Monclova in 1835. He was there when General Cos came to end the state government. Jim was one of the few able to get back to Texas safely.

When Bowie arrived, men from all over Texas were on the way to San Antonio. Jim went at once to join them. Stephen Austin was the leader of the army and Jim expected to be made an officer. Austin made no move to do that so Jim asked for a leave. Two weeks later Austin asked Jim to go with Colonel J.W. Fannin to find a camp site for the army.

Fannin and Bowie chose a place near Mission Concepcion. That night they made camp with 92 men. The next morning they woke up with over 400 Mexican soldiers around them! In the fight that followed, sixty Mexicans were killed and only one Texan. This Battle of Concepcion was the first big fight with the Mexican army. Jim was a hero! He felt sure he would be made an officer now, but Austin did not do it. Once more Bowie took a leave from the army. He went on a scouting party with Ben Milam and William Travis to the Rio Grande River.

While Bowie was gone, General Cos and his army marched to San Antonio and took over. Because the Texans were just outside the town, General Cos had a hard time getting supplies. He sent soldiers out to get grass for their horses. Bowie was just returning from the Rio Grande. He thought the Mexicans were soldiers who had come to help General Cos. He and his scouts attacked the Mexicans. They killed fifty men and took seventy horses. This time Bowie was the hero of the "Grass Fight," but he was still not made an officer.

For a third time, Jim Bowie fought bravely. He was one of the men who followed Ben Milam into San Antonio. It was hard to see the Veramendi house in the very middle of the battle. That was where he had spent many happy times with his family. Perhaps that made Jim fight harder. But Jim still was not made an officer.

Bowie went to the Texas leaders in San Felipe. He asked them if he could serve Texas. They agreed that he was much needed and Jim thought his wish soon would come true. Sam Houston was now the general of the Texas Army. Houston knew what a good fighter Bowie was and he made Jim a colonel.

Houston sent Jim orders to get some men together and go to Matamoras. Bowie never got the orders. Then Houston ordered Jim to go to the Alamo. He was to blow it up and take the cannons to Gonzales. Houston thought the Alamo was too hard to hold against the Mexican army.

If Jim had followed his orders, the history of Texas would be different. At the Alamo, Bowie found Colonel Neill and about one hundred men but no teams of horses to move the cannons. Bowie and Colonel Neill had to decide what to do. If they left the guns at the fort, the Mexican army might use the cannons on Texans. If Bowie, Colonel Neill, and the others stayed, they would need men, money, and supplies to defend the Alamo. Jim wrote to the Texas leaders. He asked for and expected to get all that was needed.

On February 12, William Travis reached the Alamo. He had been asked to bring one hundred men, but thirty was all he could get. Many people thought the fighting had ended when General Cos left San Antonio. Others were with Fannin, Dr. Grant, or Colonel Johnson planning to attack Matamoras.

Colonel Neill was called home because of sickness. That left Jim Bowie and Travis in charge. Travis had the higher rank as an officer, but the men wanted Jim Bowie for their leader. There was a bad feeling between the two leaders. At last someone came up with the answer to the problem. Travis would command the regular soldiers and Bowie would lead the rest.

For the next few days Jim was busy getting ready for the battle. He had his men pile dirt high against the walls. Then they put wooden walks on top of the dirt. This was where the soldiers would stand when the fighting started. Jim sent out for food and supplies. His men brought in thirty head of cattle and eighty bushels of corn. He made places to take care of the wounded and to store gun powder and shot. Jim was busy every moment showing his men what to do.

One day as he stood on the walkway Jim fell. It was a long fall and Jim hurt his hip very badly. He had to stay in bed, but he kept on with his plans. He got pneumonia and every day he became sicker.

On February 23, Santa Anna and his army of three thousand arrived at San Antonio. He sent word to the Texans to give up. Then Santa Anna sent out a soldier with a white flag. This meant he was willing to talk. Jim Bowie sent out one of his men with a white flag also. Nothing came of the talk except to make Colonel Travis very angry with Jim. Colonel Travis answered with a shot from a cannon.

Jim began to run high fever. For days he was out of his head. His men moved him to the place he had made for the wounded. When Bowie was able to think and speak, he asked his men to obey Travis.

On March 3, Jim was moved to a room in the church. The fever came and went but Jim had one clear idea. He wanted to do his part just like the others. He asked for two loaded pistols on his bed where he could get them. He might not be able to fight like his men, but he could lead them in bravery.

On March 6, Santa Anna's army attacked the Alamo. Jim was too weak to get out of bed. If he had lain still, he might well have lived. After all, he had married a Mexican and his name was well known among all Mexicans. But Jim had made up his mind.

Jim could hear the terrible sound of the battle coming closer and closer. He was ready. When the door to his room was thrown open, Jim called on every bit of his strength. Jim Bowie fired both pistols. Two Mexican soldiers fell dead. At once other soldiers rushed in. They stabbed Jim's body again and again. Jim Bowie was dead.

After the battle Santa Anna came to look at Jim's body. He said at first it should be buried. Then he changed his mind. It was burned along with the bodies of the other Texans. Bowie would have wanted it that way.

Jim Bowie's friends used to call him "the young lion." Jim's enemies called him "the fighting devil." To all who admire bravery, Jim Bowie was a true hero.

## William B. Travis

What kind of man do you think would want to build a town called "Liberty?" If you think it would be someone who loved freedom, you would be right. Would you believe that he was put in jail for this and held without trial? Would you be surprised to learn that this man became one of the Texas heroes who gave his life for freedom and liberty? Not if you knew his name. He was William Barrett Travis.

Travis came to Texas in 1831 on a wagon train from New Orleans. He was about twenty-two years old, married, with a son named Charles Edward. Unlike most settlers, Travis was not expecting his family to join him. He had sold all that he owned in Alabama and given it to his wife. Texas was a new beginning for him.

When Travis came to Texas, he went to Anahuac and started practicing law again. He passed the Alabama bar when he was twenty. He had also been a school teacher to pay for his training. He was smart, polite, and people liked and trusted him. As soon as possible he bought land about thirty-two miles from Anahuac. That is where he wanted to build his town called "Liberty."

Mexico sent a man named Bradburn to set up a fort at Anahuac.He was to carry out some new laws that were unfair to Texas. He also took things from the people without paying for them. When Bradburn learned that Travis was laying out a town, he jailed two men Travis had hired to survey the land. Travis tried to get them out but Bradburn would not listen. He said Travis was breaking the new law by getting more Americans to come to Texas. Then he put Travis and some of his friends in jail, too.

When Texans heard about Travis, about sixty men marched toward Anahuac. On the way they captured some of Bradburn's soldiers. The Texans said they would give up the Mexican soldiers for Travis and his friends. Bradburn agreed, but then he changed his mind. The Texans decided to fight to take Travis. They sent to Brazoria to get two cannons to attack the fort at Anahuac. There was a fight at Velasco on the way back. Several Mexicans were killed, but the Texans got the cannons.

While the other Texans were waiting at Turtle Bayou for the cannons, they wrote a paper. They listed all the bad things Bradburn had done. They stated that as settlers they had promised to obey the 1824 Constitution of Mexico. The new law of 1830 had taken away their rights and they wanted it changed. Many people in Mexico agreed with the Texans. Who do you think was their leader? General Santa Anna! The Texans said that they would give their lives for Santa Anna who was fighting for their rights and freedom.

Colonel Piedras, the commander at Nacogdoches, came to Anahuac. The Texans talked to him and gave him their paper. Colonel Piedras sent Bradburn to New Orleans and set Travis and his friends free. The Texans then went back to their homes, but all that had happened was not forgotten.

Travis moved to San Felipe where once more he set up his law office. He became friends with Stephen Austin, Sam Houston, Henry Smith, and many other leaders. He was chosen secretary to the ayuntamiento, or town council.

In July, 1832, the council wrote a

paper in support of Santa Anna. So did the ayuntamientos of San Antonio and Nacogdoches. Yet in three years Santa Anna changed from hero of freedom to dictator of Mexico! Travis had very strong feelings about all that happened in Mexico.

As a lawyer, he was interested in government. As a man who loved liberty, he was angry about the Mexican laws that were not fair. He became a leader of those who were willing to go to war over the rights of the people.

Travis knew many people and worked very hard, but he had no family to take his mind off events. That could have changed. In 1835 his wife came from Alabama with their son Charles Edward. She also brought a baby girl born a few months after Travis had left. She asked Travis to make a home for her and the children or to give her a divorce. No one knows why, but Travis gave her a divorce. She left Charles Edward with Travis and went back to Alabama with the baby girl. Travis now had his son to live for and look after, but this was a bad time to start.

In June, 1835, something happened that really made the Texans worry. General Cos, the brother-in-law of General Santa Anna sent a letter to the commander of the fort at Anahuac. He promised to send more soldiers to the fort. He also wrote that many more soldiers would come soon to "grind down" the Texans. At once, some Texans began getting ready to fight. William Travis and about twenty-five others started for Anahuac. They wanted to take the fort before other Mexican soldiers got there.

Travis and his men got a boat at Harrisburg, sailed down the San Jacinto River and across the bay to Anahuac. When they fired on the fort, many of the Mexican soldiers ran into the woods. When they came out, the soldiers gave up and it was all over! This was done with no fighting! There were no bad feelings among the soldiers. Travis and his men took all the soldiers to Harrisburg, and then sent them on to San Antonio. Before the Texans sent the Mexican soldiers there, they all had a July Fourth barbeque.

You would have thought people would be pleased with Travis, but many Texans were angry. They felt he had acted too quickly and that this would bring on war with Santa Anna and General Cos. Travis wrote a letter to defend his actions. It said in part,

"I discharged what I conceived to be my duty to my country to the best of my ability. Time alone will show whether the step was correct or not. And time will show that when the country is in danger I will show myself as patriotic and ready to serve her as those who, to save themselves, have disavowed the act and denounced me."

General Cos was angry that the Texans had found out Santa Anna's plans. He also was angry that the Texans had taken the fort at Anahuac. He sent word that Travis and other Texas leaders were to be turned over to Mexican soldiers.

The people of Texas were now divided as to what they should do. The war party was for getting ready to fight for their homes and lives. The peace party wanted to tell Santa Anna again of their loyalty to Mexico. But they were all together on one thing. They would not give up Travis and the other leaders.

Matters grew worse when the Mexican leaders sent for a small cannon at Gonzales. The cannon had been given to the people to help them fight the Indians. They decided not to give up the cannon, no matter the cost! In the fight that followed, the Texans sent the Mexican soldiers back to San Antonio – without the cannon.

At news of the fight, Texans from everwhere started to Gonzales. It was time for action, not words of peace. Travis was among those who set off at once.

Stephen Austin was chosen the leader of the Texans. The plan was to march to San Antonio and to drive all Mexican soldiers out of Texas. Austin made Travis, Ben Milam, and Jim Bowie scouts. He sent them to the Rio Grande to learn what Santa Anna was doing.

When Travis returned, he was made a major of artillery. He asked to move to the cavalry and was made lieutenant colonel. When Sam Houston became commander-in-chief of the army, he made Travis a colonel of the infantry. Houston put Travis in charge of getting men to join the army. It was a very important job, but a hard one. The trouble was that there was no way to pay the soldiers or give them clothes, food, and guns.

Colonel J.C. Neill was in command at the Alamo. He had only about one hundred men and no money, clothes, nor supplies for them. He wrote to Governor Henry Smith asking for help. General Houston knew that the Alamo could not stand against Santa Anna's army. He sent Jim Bowie with about twenty-five men to blow up the Alamo and to move the guns. But Governor Smith wanted to help Colonel Neill. He ordered Travis to get one hundred men and lead them to the Alamo.

Travis tried his best but he could get only thirty men to go with him. Soon after he arrived on February 3, Colonel Neill was called home. That caused a big problem. Both Travis and Bowie wanted to be the commander. Both men were brave and strong. Travis had the higher rank, but most of the men wanted to follow Jim Bowie. At last it was decided. The soldiers in the regular army would obey Travis. The others would obey Bowie. Travis took care of the paper work while Jim Bowie and his men tried to make the Alamo ready for battle.

Travis wrote many letters and reports. He needed the same things Colonel Neill had needed but he had even more men to look after. He wrote to Colonel Fannin who had four hundred men with him near Goliad. He begged Fannin to come at once. He wrote to all the towns asking for men and supplies. He wrote to Governor Smith and the council. His training as a lawyer and a teacher was well used. How he hoped his letters would bring help!

On February 19, the first help came to the Alamo. It was not because of the letters Travis had sent. It came in the person of Davy Crockett and some of his Tennessee boys. They had come to Texas to fight for what they knew was right. Even these few brave men made Travis feel better. Surely others would follow.

Four days later, those who came were bad news. Santa Anna and his army reached San Antonio and began firing at the Alamo. That same day James Bonham came back from Goliad. His news was a blow to the hopes of Travis. Fannin was not coming to the Alamo.

The next day Travis wrote a letter "To the People of Texas and All Americans in the World." It was a call for help in the name of liberty. As he told of the Mexican forces against him he promised that he would never surrender or retreat. He signed the letter, "Victory or death."

Travis sent this letter to Fannin in Goliad and to towns all over Texas. James Bonham went to Gonzales with the letter. Seven days later, Travis got a reply. Thirty-two men from Gonzales joined the other heroes in the Alamo.

March 3, was the last day that anyone came into or left the Alamo. The word from Fannin was the same. He would not be coming to the Alamo. James Bonham dashed into the gates knowing that there was no hope for the men inside. This was the day when each man had to know the truth.

Travis called all the men together. There were 189 men in the Alamo. He told them that no one was coming to help them. Each man knew there would be no mercy from Santa Anna. There would be no blame for anyone who chose to leave.

Then Travis drew a line on the ground with his sword. Those who chose to stay were to cross the line and stand by Travis. It was the choice of life or death. In only a moment all but one man crossed the line.

That day Travis sent one last letter to the leaders meeting at Washington-on-the-Brazos. He and others sent letters to their loved ones. Travis wrote to David Ayers. This was the man who was looking after Charles Edward while his father was gone. In the letter he said,

"Take care of my little boy. If the country should be saved, I may make him a splendid fortune; but if the country should be lost, and I should perish, he will have nothing but the proud recollection that he is the son of a man who died for his country."

Three days later on Sunday morning, William Travis died with a shot between the eyes. He had chosen to defend the one place where there was a break in the wall. He was probably one of the first men to be killed, but he was true to his word. He had promised never to surrender nor retreat. He also has left Texans the proud recollection of "a man who died for his country."

## James Bonham

You may have many friends, but what is it that makes one special – your best friend? It may be because you grew up together. It may be because you like the same things. It may be because you can talk together and be sure your friend will understand how you feel about things. It may be because you can count on your friend.

James Bonham was the best friend of William Travis for all those reasons. James and William were both born in Red Bank, South Carolina. Their families were neighbors and the boys went to the same school and played together. They both were great talkers and were ready to fight for what they thought was right.

It was a sad day for James when William's family moved to Alabama. James was nine years old at the time, but he did not want to lose his best friend. He and William promised to write to each other and they did. In this way they kept up with what the other was doing and thinking.

James went to South Carolina College, but he did not finish. He and his class thought the rules were too hard and the food too bad. They asked that both be changed. The college told the class to leave if it did not like things as they were. James and his whole class left but James did not stop learning. He began studying law. About the same time William Travis was studying law in Alabama. Even though they were apart, the friends still liked the same things.

James opened his law office in Pendleton, South Carolina. In two years he was working closely with the Governor of the state. He also was made colonel of artillery in the state militia. He was making a name for himself as a lawyer, too, but one day he got into trouble. When a lawyer said bad things about a lady on trial, James threw the man out of court. The judge told James he would have to pay a fine for his actions. James refused to pay so he went to jail. Both James and Travis in Texas went to jail because they tried to stand up for the rights of others.

Bonham decided to move to Montgomery, Alabama, and open a law office there. All was going well until he got a letter from Travis in Texas. Travis told him that Texas was "the land of the future." He also told him that "stirring things were afoot." He asked him to "come out to Texas and take a hand in the affairs." This invitation from Travis was all that it took.

James closed his law office, went back to South Carolina to tell his mother goodbye and then went to Mobile, Alabama. There, with two other men, Bonham got together thirty men to go with them to Texas. They called themselves the "Mobile Grays" and arrived in Texas on December 12, 1835. General Cos had just given up the Alamo and was on his way to Mexico, but it was not all over.

General Houston was trying to raise an army for the fighting to come. Travis lost no time in having Bonham meet the General and other Texas leaders. On December 20, Houston made Bonham lieutenant of the cavalry and asked him to get others to join. Houston also asked the Council to make Bonham a major but the Council did not act.

On January 17, Bonham went with Jim Bowie to the Alamo. Their orders were to move the cannons and blow up the buildings. James was there when Travis arrived with thirty men on February 3. How glad the friends were to be together. Travis needed someone he could trust to help him do what he felt he must do.

Travis knew that Colonel James Fannin had about four hundred men with him at Goliad. He knew that the Alamo could not be held without more men and supplies. He sent James Bonham to Colonel Fannin to ask him to come at once. Bonham left the Alamo on February 16.

Bonham used all of his power to get Fannin to leave Goliad for the Alamo. No matter how hard he tried, Bonham could not get Fannin to make up his mind to go. Perhaps Fannin thought he could stop Santa Anna from ever getting to the Alamo. Perhaps he did not want to give up his command to another. Perhaps he was just too interested in his own plans and problems. Bonham had to go back to the Alamo with no word of help.

The day Bonham returned was the same day Santa Anna's army reached San Antonio. Travis wrote letters to the Texas leaders, to every town, to General Houston and to Colonel Fannin. Once more he asked his friend James to go to Goliad, Gonzales, and other places. Both men knew this trip would be much harder than the last one. The Mexicans were watching the Alamo to keep anyone from going in or out. The country was full of Mexican scouts and other soldiers on the way to San Antonio. Even the Texans might shoot anyone who could be an enemy. Yet Bonham did not wait one moment to agree to go and do his best.

Travis took a white handkerchief from his pocket. He gave it to his friend and told him to tie it on his hat when he came back to the Alamo. This would be a sign to the Texans to open the gates. Without this sign, the gates would stay shut.

Bonham rode hard to get the letters to all those to whom Travis had written. He went first to Fannin at Goliad. This time Fannin decided to go to Travis' aid. He started his march on February 28, with his cannons mounted on wagons. The troops had only gone about two hundred yards before the wagons broke down. Fannin called his officers together. They decided to turn back to Goliad. After that, there was no changing Fannin's mind.

Bonham went to Gonzales and to other towns. In only one place did he find anyone willing to go to the Alamo. Captain Albert Martin and thirty-one men from Gonzales started at once and reached the Alamo on March 1.

Bonham delivered his last letter. He was a big, strong man but he and his horse were very tired. His friends begged him to rest. They all knew there was no way the Alamo could stand against Santa Anna's army. Bonham would not listen. His job was not done. He felt he must tell his friends all that he had learned wherever he stopped. He also knew his friend needed him.

On the morning of March 3, Bohnam got out the white handkerchief Travis had given him. He put it on his hat where it would be easy to see. Then he got ready to make a run for the Alamo.

The Mexicans had found the way the Texans had been getting in and out of the Alamo. Since this happened at night, they left only a few soldiers on guard during the day.

Bonham chose the way that was closest to the gate. He rode quietly through the cottonwood trees until he came to the open ground. Then he spurred his horse and dashed for the Alamo gate.

The Mexicans were taken by surprise! Could this be a Texan? It was eleven o'clock in the morning! They grabbed their guns and began to yell and fire at the flying horseman. At the same time the guards in the Alamo saw a man on a horse galloping toward them. On his hat was a white handkerchief. It was the sign they had been looking for. At once they swung open the gate just wide enough for the horse and rider to slip inside. A cheer went up from the Alamo. Surely this was a good sign.

Bonham went at once to talk to Travis. What he had to do was harder than anything he had been through. He told Travis that no help was coming from Fannin or anyone else. They both knew what that meant.

Later that day Travis got all the men together. He told them what they had all feared was the truth. He said there would be no blame on those who chose to leave. Those who stayed would fight Santa Anna's army as long as possible. James Bonham was one of those who chose to stay.

James Bonham was the last man to enter the Alamo, but two men left. One man left with no blame. The other carried letters Travis and the others had written to their families and leaders at Washington-on-the-Brazos. This time James Bonham did not carry the letters.

Travis was one of the first men killed on Sunday morning, March 6. He was firing the cannon at the break in the Alamo wall. James Bonham was one of the last men to be killed at the Alamo. He, too, was firing a cannon – this one on top of the chapel.

Throughout their lives, James Bonham and William Travis had done many of the same things. They had been able to talk together and understand the other's feeling. They had stood up for the rights of others. There could be no greater proof of their friendship. James Bonham had chosen to die for and with his best friend.

## Davy Crockett

Many people like to tell tall tales. They make up stories that surprise their friends and make them laugh. When a man does things that are as exciting and wonderful as his stories, he becomes a legend. Such a man was Davy Crockett.

Davy heard many stories and tall tales when he was a boy. His father had an inn on the western side of the Blue Ridge Mountains in Tennessee. This was wild country with very few settlers. When travelers came to the inn, everyone wanted them to talk. They brought news from the other side of the mountain. Best of all were the stories they had heard and passed on. Someone else would tell another story and so the evening would pass. Many of the stories were about the wild animals in the forests and hunters. Davy loved to listen to them!

There was little for Davy to do around the inn. There was no school for him to attend. Besides, Davy wanted to explore the forest. He wanted to see the wild animals and learn their ways. He wanted to become a hunter.

When Davy was eight years old, his father gave him a gun. He could have only a single load of ball and powder each day. He was to bring home game for supper or go hungry. There were very few days that he did not eat. He learned the call of the birds, the sounds of animals, and the signs of the forest. These were happy days for young Davy.

In the summer when Davy was twelve years old, his father let him drive a herd of cattle to Virginia. When he got home, a new school was just starting. Davy and his brothers and sisters all went, but this did not last long for Davy. He got in a fight with a bully and beat the boy up.

The schoolmaster said Davy could not come back to school unless he had a whipping, too. Davy decided to run away. He left with a man driving another herd of cattle to Virginia.

For the next three years Davy worked at whatever he could find to do. Most of the time he helped farmers. For a while he helped make beaver hats for gentlemen. He had a chance to sail as a cabin boy to London from Baltimore, but he wanted to go home. This time when he got to the inn, his family hardly knew him. He was no longer a boy.

Times had been hard for the Crocketts. Davy's father owed a debt to a neighbor. The neighbor agreed to let Davy work for him to repay the debt. Davy was glad to help his family in this way. There was another person to whom the family owed money. This was a Quaker and he, too, let Davy work to repay the debt. The Quaker was a kind man and he sent Davy to school to learn to read. This was the only real schooling Davy ever had.

Davy worked hard, but there were times of fun, too. In the fall when the grain was reaped and the flax pulled, there was a frolic. After the work was done, the dancing began. Davy loved to dance and all of his life he danced whenever he had the chance.

It was at a frolic that Davy met Polly Finley. She was pretty, little, with blond hair and she liked to dance as much as Davy. They danced Irish and English reels and sang and played play-party games. Before the night was over they were engaged.

Davy's parents agreed that he could marry. He worked for six months to get a good horse and he rented a farm where

they could live. Davy and Polly were married three days before he was nineteen and they were very happy.

Davy really was not a farmer. He wanted to hunt and he felt he could make more for his family by hunting. The country where they were living was filling up with settlers and they had driven the game away. Davy and Polly decided to push on into the wilderness. With Polly and their two little boys riding on their horse and Davy walking, they set out for Elk River country across the Cumberland Mountains.

There were few bears in Elk River country, but plenty of wild turkeys, possums and raccoons. Raccoon skins were worth a lot of money. Because he killed so many, Davy began to have stories told about himself. It was said that he could out grin a raccoon, but he was a great hunter of other animals, too. In winter, his family had plenty of warm fox fur caps, coonskin coats, deerskin leggins, and hunting shirts. There were bearskin rugs and soft furs to cover the beds.

When a hurricane came through the Elk River country, it tore the roof off Davy's cabin and twisted the rafters. Davy took this as a sign he should move on near the Mississippi Territory. This was where there were many panthers. It was also Indian land. The Cherokees were peace-loving but the Creeks wanted to make war.

When word came that the Creeks had attacked Fort Mims in Alabama, a call went out for volunteers. Davy was the second man to sign up for sixty days. Like the others in his company, he went, riding his own horse, carrying his own rifle, and dressed for hunting.

Crockett was made a scout to go into Creek country to learn what the Indians were planning. Not all the tribes were on the war path. The Cherokees wanted no part of the fighting against the white man. They, too, were threatened by the Creeks.

While Davy was scouting, General Andrew Jackson was trying to get supplies for the men. Food was scarce and the men grew restless and hungry. Davy Crockett told tales and stories around the campfire to help the men forget their troubles. He also hunted to get food for the men. He was a friend to all of them.

At the end of the war, Davy was at the Indian Holy Ground where the treaty was made. The Indians had a treaty signed by George Washington that was not to be broken, but General Jackson broke it. He made the Indians give up part of their land. The rest they were to keep forever. Davy did not think it right to break the treaty.

Soon after Davy came home, Polly grew sick and died. Davy was so sad he could not stay in the cabin where he and Polly had lived. This time with his children he set off for new land on Shoal Creek. There he met Elizabeth Patton whose husband had been killed in the Creek War. She had small children also. Davy asked her to marry him and they made a good life together.

In this wild country, many bad men came to live. Davy was made colonel of the militia to protect the settlers. He also became the judge of the county. Davy did not know how to write, but he read all he could. He practiced writing every night

until he had a good handwriting. He signed all his papers, "Be sure you're right, then go ahead." He was a wise and fair judge.

In 1821 Davy was asked to run for the state legislature. He did not know how to "make a speech," but he told a story or two to show how he felt about things. The people liked his ways and what he said so he was elected twice to the legislature. Some of the other lawmakers called him the "gentleman from the cane." This was because of the wilderness called the Shakes where he was now living. It was the finest hunting country Davy had ever found. One year alone he shot 108 bears. No wonder he was known as the greatest bear hunter!

During these years times were hard. Skins did not sell for much and Davy needed another way to make money for his family. He hired some men to cut wood into staves to make barrels. He built two flatboats to take the staves to New Orleans.

Davy knew nothing about piloting a boat so he hired someone. This man knew little more than Davy. Even if he had, there would have been trouble. When the boats came to the Mississippi River it was flooding and out of its banks.

One night the boats ran into a pile of trees and logs that overturned the flatboats. All thirty thousand staves that Davy had worked hard to make floated down the river. Davy could have been angry, but he was glad that he and his men were alive.

In 1825 Davy was asked to run for Congress. He felt that he did not know enough to do a good job. He did not get elected, but two years later he ran again and won. He took the seat of Sam Houston who became Governor of Tennessee.

Andrew Jackson was running for president in 1828 and Crockett wanted to see him elected. The "Coonskin Congressman" as Davy was called in Washington showed his feelings when he was asked who he was.

"I'm Davy Crockett, fresh from the backwoods, half-horse, half-alligator, a little touched with snapping turtle. I can wade the Mississippi, leap the Ohio, ride a streak of lightning, slip without a scratch down a honey locust, whip my weight in wildcats, hug a bear too close for comfort and eat any man opposed to Jackson."

Congress had never known anyone like Crockett. Because of his terms in the Tennessee Legislature, he knew how laws were passed. He spoke out in his own way for what he thought was right.

The second time he went to Congress, Davy spoke against a land law. It would take land away from poor people. President Jackson had been a land speculator and he was for the bill. This was the first break between the men, but another was coming. President Jackson wanted to break the treaty with the Indians that he himself had made after the Creek War! He now wanted to take the lands that had been promised forever. Davy fought long and hard to keep this from happening but he lost. He also lost his election to Congress in 1831 but was back again in 1833. He was more popular now than ever.

The newspapers were full of things Davy said and did. Books came out that claimed to tell about his life. Davy himself had learned to write well and to set things straight he wrote a book. It was called *Narrative of the Life of Davy Crockett, of the State of Tennessee, Written by Himself.* He said that a friend helped him because he was a poor speller. He wrote another book called *An Account of Col. Crockett's Tour of the North and Down East.*

In the election of 1835 Davy failed to win. All those whom he had spoken against came together to defeat him. He was not without friends, but now he was at a turning point in his life. Too much had changed for him to go back to hunting and farming in the Shakes. It was time for him to move again. This time it would not be in Tennessee. Davy Crockett was going to Texas.

On October 31, 1835, Davy wrote to his brother that he was leaving to explore Texas. In the letter he said four other men were going with him. His plan was to go through Arkansas.

When Crockett reached Little Rock, people recognized him. They gave him a dinner and sent him on his way with many new friends. Everywhere he went he asked for news of Texas. He took time to explore some land along the Red River and to visit Indians. He had been friends with Indians all of his life. He wanted to choose the best place to settle his family.

When Davy and his friends came to San Augustine, cannons were fired in his honor. His group pressed on to Nacogdoches where a banquet was being held for the former governor of Coahuila-Texas. Crockett and his friends were invited to join the fun.

The very next day Davy signed a paper to support any "republican" government in Texas. Four days later, on January 9, 1836, Davy wrote to two of his children. He told of the wonderful country and said he wanted to settle near the Red River. He had signed as a volunteer for six months and was to set out for the Rio Grande River. He hoped to be chosen to help form the Constitution for Texas and he "rejoiced at his fate."

On February 18, Davy Crockett and about twelve other Tennessee Volunteers rode into San Antonio. He was greeted with delight by all present. That night there was a feast for Davy and on the 23rd there was a fandango. This was somewhat different from a frolic, but Davy danced with just as much pleasure.

The next day Santa Anna and his army took over San Antonio. Davy and his men busied themselves getting the Alamo ready for battle. Each took turns standing guard on the wooden walks inside the building. At night Davy kept their spirits high with his tales of hunting. He even tried to play the fiddle to make things better.

On the twelfth day, when the men in

the Alamo knew their fate, Travis asked Davy and his men to defend the stockade before the chapel. Davy was to take command if Travis should fall.

At the first sound of the enemy on the morning of the sixth, Davy and his men took their places. With deadly aim they drove the enemy back, not once but twice. Davy's shooting had never been sharper.

As the Mexicans rushed the Alamo the third time, Davy was handed a loaded gun, as quickly as he had fired. This time there was no stopping the enemy. They climbed ladders and poured into the Alamo, firing as they came. The Texans dropped where they stood.

Davy Crockett and his men stood their ground as long as possible. When the guns could no longer be fired they became clubs. When at last Davy was shot, he fell across a pile of the enemy who had tried to get to him.

All of the Texans who died at the Alamo were heros. Many of them had lived in Texas long enough to be fighting for their families and homes. Others were brave men who had come to fight in the cause of right. Such a man was Davy Crockett. He was a legend for what he did as a hunter. He was a legend for the stories he told and those he caused to be told. Mostly he was a legend for living up to his rule.

"I leave this rule for others when I'm dead, 'be always sure you're right, then go ahead.'"

## *Jose Antonio Navarro*

The year 1813 was one Jose Antonio Navarro would never forget. As a young man of eighteen he joined the Republican Army of the North led by Augustus Magee and Bernardo Gutierrez. The Republicans, as they called themselves, wanted to free Texas from Spanish rulers called "Royalists." Then the Republicans planned to march to Mexico and help Mexico win independence from Spain.

At first all went well and for three and one-half months Texas was free of Spanish rule. Then General Joaquin de Arrendondo suddenly appeared from Mexico with two thousand soldiers. Near the Medina River, the General's soldiers fought the Republicans and almost wiped out the entire force of fourteen hundred men. Navarro was one of the lucky ones. He got away to Louisiana, but he did not see Texas again for three years.

When Navarro came back to his home in San Antonio, he found things had changed. Many people had left Texas just as he had, but they never came back. Others had been killed, either by General Arrendondo or by the Indians. There were very few white people left in the whole of Texas, but Navarro hoped this would change.

Five years later Navarro met Stephen Austin. The two men were about the same age and they liked each other at once. Navarro was glad Stephen planned to bring new settlers to Texas and he promised to do all he could to help his new friend. He was to have that chance often, and he never let his friend down.

In 1824 Coahuila and Texas became a state of Mexico. Jose was chosen to go to the state legislature where he spoke for laws that would help the settlers. In

Mexico, planters used Indians to work the fields, but the Mexican government passed laws against people in Texas having slaves. Navarro knew the settlers needed slaves to clear and plant their land so he defended their rights in this and other matters. Because of his actions, Navarro was known as an American-ized Texan.

Other Americans wanted to get grants of land like Austin's so Navarro helped them. Because of Navarro, Ben Milam, General Arthur Wavell, and Green Dewitt all became empresarios. Each of these men hoped to bring families to live on their lands, but Navarro was interested in land for ranching. In 1825, Navarro himself got grants in the present counties of Atascosa, Karnes, Guadalupe, Travis, and Bastrop.

Ranching was not Navarro's only business. He ran a store and practiced law while he took part in helping the country in many ways. Everything he did added to his understanding of Texas and the people living here. He talked to Mexicans to help them get along well with the Anglo neighbors while he did the same for the settlers in teaching them about the Mexicans.

In 1833 the State of Coahuila-Texas asked Navarro to be ready to go to the Congress in Mexico City if needed. The next year he was the land commissioner for the area around San Antonio. In 1835 Jose was made the senator from Coahuila-Texas to the Mexican Congress, but he pretended to be ill. He did not want to be part of the trouble Santa Anna was stirring up in Mexico.

For several years the people of Texas had wanted to be a separate state. They liked living under the Mexican Constitution of 1824, but they wanted their own state government. When Santa Anna became dictator, he did away with the Constitution. He sent people to Texas to collect taxes on everything that was brought into the country. He also sent soldiers to see that the taxes were paid.

The people of Texas knew that no longer was it a question of becoming a separate state of Mexico. It was time to think about independence. Every town in Texas was asked to send its wisest men to a convention. Jose Navarro was one of the four men who went from San Antonio.

The Convention met on March 1, 1836, at Washington-on-the-Brazos. It could hardly be called a town, for it had only a few cabins and there were stumps of trees standing in its only street. The Convention met in a rented house that was only half built with pieces of cloth over the windows to shut out the cold. It would be hard to find a more uncomfortable place, but the men who came did not mind. They knew the work to be done for Texas was more important than any before.

Of the fifty-nine men present, two had been born in Texas. One of them was Navarro. Word came to the Convention of the need for men to go to the Alamo to help Travis. They also knew that Texans under Dr. Grant and Colonel Johnston had been killed near San Patricio. Some of the men thought the Convention should end and all go to the fight, but Sam Houston felt Texas needed a government first. A committee was chosen to write a declaration of independence from Mexico. The very next day, March 2, 1836, the declaration was read and signed by everyone at the Convention.

Jose Antonio Navarro was the seventh man to sign.

The next job of the Convention was writing a constitution for the new Republic of Texas. One man from each town was chosen and Navarro was one of the twenty-one men given this important job. For two weeks this group worked night and day. Finally in the early morning of March 16, the job was done. The Convention voted to accept the constitution and then elected new officers of the government. The next day the officers left for Harrisburg, while the other men of the convention left to do their part in the war.

When peace came, Navarro went back to San Antonio. He served in the third Congress of the Republic and was elected to the fourth but he was too ill to go.

In 1841 President Lamar asked Navarro to be the commissioner on the Santa Fe Expedition. Jose's job was to get the people of Santa Fe to join the Republic of Texas. Navarro really did not want to go, but he could not turn down the President.

From the very first the Santa Fe Expedition was in trouble. The leaders lost their way and there was not enough food nor supplies for the men. The Mexicans found out about the Expedition and captured the group on October 5, 1841. Navarro was to have special treatment, but the kind he got was not what had been agreed upon. He was separated from the rest of the men in Mexico City and put in Acordada Prison. Under orders from Santa Anna, Navarro was tried and sentenced to death, but, through friends, his sentence was changed to life in prison. He was sent to the dungeon of San Juan de Ullo with little hope of ever

being free.

For three long years Navarro stayed in the dungeon. At last, on December 18, 1844, friends of Navarro were able to get a parole for him to stay in Vera Cruz. Vera Cruz was a busy port where ships from many countries landed. A British ship was about to sail for Cuba and Navarro saw his chance to escape. He made good plans and was happy to leave the shores of Mexico. From Cuba he took another ship to New Orleans where he landed on January 18, 1845. Exactly one month later he reached his ranch home near

Geronimo. Texas had never looked so good to him.

Anson Jones called a convention in July, 1845, to decide whether Texas should join the United States or stay an independent country. Mexico had at last signed a treaty of peace, but the people of Texas wanted to become a state of the Union. This led to the writing of a constitution. This was the second time Navarro had helped write a constitution. He was the only Mexican born in Texas to have had two such important jobs.

The state constitution divided the

land into counties. In April, 1846, Navarro county was named in honor of this brave Texan and its county seat was called "Corsicana." This name came from the Island of Corsica where Navarro's father had been born. Navarro was honored by all the people of Texas for all he had done and the hardships he had lived through.

From 1846 to 1849 Navarro was a senator in the State Legislature. Although he was always ready to help, he spent the next years looking after his family of seven children and ranching. He gave the land in Atascosa County for a county seat to be called "Navatasco," but the town of Pleasanton became the county seat.

In 1861, Navarro went again to the capitol in Austin. This time he voted for Texas to leave the United States and join the Confederacy. All four of his sons fought in the Confederate army. Navarro, as always, did what he could to support the cause he believed in.

Ten years later Navarro died. He was a man who had seen many great changes and had played a part in building Texas into greatness. Always for independence, Navarro had fought against Spain and supported Texas against Mexico. He voted to leave the Union he had once voted to join. He helped write two constitutions and saw Texas change from a state to a republic and back to a state again. He served Texas in whatever way he was asked if he thought it right. A man born on Texas soil, he had first claim to being called "a true Texan."

## James W. Fannin

How many decisions have you made today? Probably a lot more than you think. You make some decisions almost without thinking about them. Others may take time and a great deal of thought. Even when you decide not to make a decision you are making one!

Leaders are people chosen to make decisions. Sometimes they make wise choices. At other times their decisions are poor. Sometimes the decision may be right, but it may be made at the wrong time. It is not easy to make up your mind when the decision affects others.

James Fannin was a brave man who had to make some hard decisions. He had come to Texas in 1834 and had bought a plantation near Velasco. Almost from the first he thought Texas should be free. When the call for help came from Gonzales, Fannin was one of the first to go. He was the captain of the Brazos Guards.

After Stephen Austin was made commander of the volunteer army, Fannin and Jim Bowie were chosen to find a campsite near San Antonio. They found a place near the Mission Concepcion. The next morning they also found four hundred Mexican soldiers around them. In the battle that followed, sixty Mexicans were killed and only one Texan. This showed what good officers Fannin and Bowie were.

Fannin had gone to West Point for two years as a young man. He felt that Texas should have a regular, full-time army. He left the volunteers at San Antonio on November 22. He hoped to get the Governor and the Council to act on his idea. He did not know that they had made Sam Houston commander-in-chief a few days earlier.

Sam Houston had been told to set up and raise a regular army. He was also to get militia and rangers to protect the people from Indians and other dangers. It was a big job and Houston needed good men he could count on. He made Fannin a colonel in the regular army and sent him to Velasco as commander. Fannin was to try to get men to join the regular army. The government also asked Fannin to get men, guns, and supplies for the volunteers at San Antonio. Fannin did not decide which job was more important. He tried to do both.

After General Cos was defeated at the Alamo, many Texans went home. They thought the fighting was over. Others wanted to take the battle to Mexico. There were stories of numbers of Mexicans who were against Santa Anna. Some people thought that, if the Texans took Matamoros, many Mexicans would join the Texans.

To men from the states who had come to fight, this sounded like a fine idea. Before long several hundred men were on their way west. On December 30, Houston ordered Fannin to go to Copano. Men were gathering there getting ready to march to Matamoros. Fannin was not to start for Matamoros without orders. He was to wait until General Houston arrived.

Many people in Texas did not think fighting at Matamoros was a good idea. The Governor and the Council did not agree on this as well as other things. At the very time Texas needed a strong government, it was weak.

On January 7, the Council made Fannin an "agent." They said he could raise money, volunteers, supplies, and even begin fighting if he wanted to. He could let other people raise money and supplies for him. He was to report either to General Houston, the Governor, or the Council.

What should Fannin do? He was a colonel in the regular army under General Houston. If he did what the Council said, he would be more powerful than the Governor or Houston. On January 8 Fannin sent out a call for volunteers to join him at San Patricio.

The Governor was very angry. The Council did not have the right to do this! General Houston knew what this meant, also. He asked the Governor to give him a leave from his command. The Governor gave him until March 1.

On February 1, General Urrea reached Matamoros with several hundred men. When this news reached Fannin, he moved his headquarters to Goliad. The fort there needed much work so he set the volunteers to making the fort strong. Fannin called it "Fort Defiance." Fannin now was the commander of all volunteers.

On February 17, a soldier who was not coming to join Fannin reached the fort. It was James Bonham, the trusted friend of William Travis. Bonham came to ask Fannin to send help to the Alamo. Fannin had almost five hundred men. Some of them had been at the Alamo and they knew it would take men to defend it. Bonham did all that he could, but Fannin would not give him a decision.

On February 25, Fannin got a letter from Travis. Once more he begged for help. Fannin had to decide what to do. He wanted to help Travis but he knew General Urrea was heading for Texas. Fannin had not been able to get much food nor supplies for his men. Many of them were ragged and their shoes were worn through. Would it be better to stay in Goliad and fight the Mexicans there or go to San Antonio? For two days he tried to decide.

At last on February 28, Fannin set out for the Alamo with three hundred men. The soldiers had gone only about two hundred yards when a wagon broke down. Everyone stopped. While they were in the middle of the road five men dashed up. Colonel Johnson and the other four had been at San Patricio. General Urrea had come suddenly upon the men there and these five were the only Texans left. It was just a matter of time before General Urrea would reach Refugio and then Goliad.

This time it did not take Fannin long to decide what to do. He turned back to Fort Defiance at once. He and his men started doing more work on the fort.

General Houston went to Washington-on-the-Brazos on March 1. On March 4, and for the third time, he was made commander-in-chief of all forces. On March 11, from his headquarters at Gonzales, Houston ordered Fannin to retreat to Victoria at once. Fannin was to take what guns he could, sink the others in the river, and blow up the fort.

On March 12, Fannin sent Captain King and twenty-eight men to Refugio. There were families in the mission with no way to leave. Captain King was to come back to Goliad quickly, but he did not. He waited several hours. By that time some of General Urrea's soldiers had entered the town.

When King failed to reach the fort, Fannin was afraid something had

happened. He sent Major Ward with one hundred men to Refugio that same night. Major Ward was able to get into the mission. He sent Captain King to scout the enemy, but Captain King never came back.

The next day Major Ward fought about six hundred Mexicans, killing about two hundred. Only three Texans were wounded. Ward knew more Mexican soldiers would soon come. He and his men slipped out of the mission at night and started for Goliad. They stuck to the woods and swamps so the Mexican cavalry could not get to them.

On March 14, Fannin got his orders from General Houston. He sent a message at once to Major Ward telling him to come. He sent a second and then a third message, but he got no word. On March 17, Fannin learned that Urrea was on his way to Goliad.

Fannin made ready for battle. On

March 18, Fannin's cannons blasted the enemy and the Mexicans made a fast retreat. Fannin also got news of Ward so he made plans to leave the fort. The cannons were mounted on ox carts and the buildings burned. Fannin even did away with food to be able to carry the cannons. His force of about three hundred men left on the morning of March 19. About ten o'clock, the last of the soldiers and the wagons crossed the river.

About eight miles from Goliad, Fannin ordered a halt to let the oxen graze. Some of his officers thought they should push on to the Coleto. Fannin did not believe the enemy was near so he did not hurry. About an hour later the march began again. Suddenly Mexican cavalry began coming out of the woods toward the right and the rear of the Texans. Some woods were about a mile ahead of Fannin's men. They hurried their pace, but the Mexicans formed a line between the Texans and the trees. There was nothing to do but prepare for battle.

The Texans were in an open prairie. They quickly formed a square and began to fire with cannons and guns at the enemy all about them. All that day until dark the battle went on. General Urrea had an army of about twelve hundred soldiers. He also had seven hundred cavalry.

The Texans fought bravely. They fired their cannons until they became too hot to use. There was no water to cool them down. The only defense was from rifles and hand guns, yet only seven Texans were killed. About sixty were badly wounded.

That night the cries and moans of wounded men and animals made a terrible sound. The Texans were without water and there was no way to get any. Gun powder was running low. There was no hope of help from anywhere. There was nothing for the Texans to do but give up.

The next morning, March 20, the Texans raised a white flag. Fannin had been wounded but he met with the Mexicans to talk of terms. A paper was written that made the Texans prisoners of war. The Texans piled up their arms and were marched back to Goliad. The wounded were brought two days later.

On March 23, Fannin went to Copano with a colonel in the Mexican army. They were trying to find a ship but there was none. As prisoners of war, Fannin thought they would all be sent out of the country. They could never again take up arms against Mexico. Colonel Fannin returned to Goliad on March 26.

The same night a special message came to Colonel Portilla. He was the officer in charge of the prisoners. Sometime earlier Santa Anna had passed a law. It stated that anyone carrying arms against Mexico would be treated as a pirate and shot. Santa Anna's orders were clear. Kill the Texans.

The next day was Palm Sunday. At dawn the Texans were made to get up and form three lines. Some were told they were to march to Copano. Others were told they were to help kill some cattle for food. Still others were told they were to be moved to make room for Santa Anna's men. Each line was marched off down a different road.

Suddenly the Mexicans guarding the prisoners called a halt. The Texans were told to sit down with their backs to the

guards. Then at a word from an officer the Mexican soldiers fired. Most of the Texans were killed at once. A few were able to get away. An hour later the wounded men were taken out and shot. Three hundred and thirty men were murdered in cold blood!

Fannin was the last to die and he died bravely as a soldier. He gave his watch to an officer and asked that it be sent to his family. He asked that he be shot in the chest and not in the head. He asked that his body be buried. Then he put a handkerchief over his eyes and waited for the shot that would take his life. Not one of his wishes was carried out.

The only Texans who were spared were the doctors and their helpers. Eighty men who had just arrived at Victoria were spared because they had no guns with them. Perhaps twenty-five others escaped from the shooting.

When the people of Texas learned what had happened, they were shocked. With two great defeats so close together there was fear everywhere. Many Texans gathered their children and goods to run to safety. Others who had not joined in the fighting started for the army. People everywhere were with the Texans in their fight for freedom.

Would things have been different at the Alamo if Fannin had gone earlier? Would the Texans have been better off if Fannin had obeyed Houston's orders at once? By deciding to send help to Refugio, Fannin lost four days. There is no doubt that Fannin was a brave soldier and a kind man. Whether he made the right decisions and if other choices would have made a difference, there is no way of knowing.

## David Burnet

"Run for your lives! Santa Anna is coming! There's no time to lose! Leave Harrisburg now!"

David Burnet looked at the man who had just shouted these words. Then he turned to the men in the room behind him.

"We must leave at once. Meet me at Morgan's Point. If we have to, we can go on to Galveston Island."

At once men began to gather papers from the table where they were working. David Burnet was the last to leave the room. He was worried about his family near Lynch's Ferry, but Texas was on his mind. As President ad interim, he knew the government must continue if Texas was to be free.

The street was already full of people running toward the dock. A little ship named "Cayuga" was about to sail for Anahuac. Everyone crowded on except the two Borden brothers who ran a newspaper. They had brought their press from San Felipe and they wanted to get out a paper before they left.

When the Cayuga stopped at Morgan's Point, David got off. He sent the rest of the government to Galveston, but he had work to do. He sent a scout to General Houston to find out where he was. He also made plans to get to Galveston if he had to leave in a hurry. Two of his friends, Mr. and Mrs. Gilbert Brooks, had a small sailboat. They said they would take David to Galveston.

On the morning of April 17, 1836, the scout came back. He had not been able to reach General Houston because the Mexican army was marching to Morgan's Point. David knew he must leave at once, but there was one problem. He had many important papers with him. He did not want the papers with him if the enemy captured him. He was afraid to take them with him on the boat because they might get washed overboard. It would not be wise to leave them in a house which might be burned. He and Gilbert Brooks decided to bury the papers under a big tree in Brooks' yard.

As David and his friend put the last earth in place over the papers, they heard the sound of horses. Mrs. Brooks was already in the boat. The two men jumped in and pushed away from the shore. Brooks rowed hard until the sail was up and the wind pushed the boat along. Mexican horsemen raced along the shore following the boat.

At one time the wind pushed the boat near the shore. The Mexicans raised their guns to fire. Mrs. Brooks stood up in the boat and spread her skirts over Burnet and her husband. The Mexicans stopped and then let their guns drop. Just then the wind shifted and the boat headed for deeper water. As the boat pulled away, the soldiers fired, but their shots fell short. The horsemen slowed their pace and then stopped. Burnet and his friends had escaped.

Being the president was not always this exciting. It was a very hard job. Burnet had to hold the country together while the war was going on. Most Texans were running for their lives to get to Louisiana. Burnet had no money to buy things for the army or to pay the soldiers. He did not even have a capital. The capital was wherever the president happened to be!

When Santa Anna was defeated at San Jacinto, Burnet and his cabinet had to decide what to do with him. They also had to make a peace treaty with Mexico. Burnet did not know how to make a treaty, but he ended up making two. One was a public treaty and the other was secret. The first promised the end of the war. Santa Anna promised to get Mexico to accept Texas as free in the secret treaty. The Texans wanted the Rio Grande River to be the line between the two countries.

Many men from the United States had started for Texas before the Battle of San Jacinto. When they reached Texas, the war was over. They wanted to go on to Mexico and fight. They also wanted Santa Anna killed. President Burnet put Santa Anna on a ship for Mexico but the soldiers found out. They made Burnet take Santa Anna off the ship and hold him a prisoner.

The soldiers also wanted Burnet to step down and let the army take over the country. Burnet would not do it. He was the ad interim president and he would stay until the people could vote on the constitution.

The words "ad interim" show that something is to last only a little while. Burnet was president from March 17, 1836, to October 22, 1836. He called for a vote on the constitution on September 5, 1836. The people voted for the constitution. They also elected Sam Houston as the first president of the Republic of Texas.

Burnet was glad to let Houston take over. There were still many problems, but with the people behind him, Sam Houston could face them. Perhaps Burnet wanted time to think about all that had happened to him in his life.

David, the youngest of eight children, had been born in New Jersey. After his mother and father had died, he lived with his older brother. At sixteen he went to work in a counting house. When he learned it was about to fail, he put up all his money to try to save it. The counting house failed anyway and David had lost everything.

Burnet learned that Francisco Miranda was getting men together to try to free Venezuela. Burnet joined the group and was made a lieutenant. Miranda put him in charge of a boatload of fighting men. Burnet gave the order to fire the first shot for South American freedom.

When David was twenty-five, he went to Natchitoches, Louisiana. He set up a trading post and hoped to make money. Before long Burnet became sick. He might have grown weak from living in Venezuela, for many of the soldiers had died from yellow fever. This was not Burnet's illness. He had tuberculosis.

When the trading post failed, Burnet started to Texas, sick and down hearted. As he rode near the Colorado River, David fell from his horse. Sometime later he was found by some Comanches. They picked him up and took him with them. For almost two years Burnet lived with the Indians. They nursed him and made him well again.

Burnet decided to study law. He went to Ohio and set up his office, but he made trips back to Texas during the next six years. At last in 1826, Burnet came to Texas to live. He met many men with whom he would work when he was president. He went to Saltillo and got a grant of land next to the grants of

Lorenzo de Zavala and Joseph Vehlein. Burnet did not have money to work his grant. He turned it over to the Galveston Bay and Texas Land Company.

In 1830 Burnet married Hannah Este from New York. He brought her to Texas and they lived on a plantation near Lynch's Ferry. He wanted to farm, but he was not very successful.

When the Convention of 1833 was called, David was given a big job. He was asked to write a paper telling why Texas wanted to be a separate state of Mexico. At that time Texas and Coahuila were one state. The capitol was at Saltillo and this was far from the people of Texas. The Coahuila members did not understand the Texans, their needs, nor their ways. Texas was not trying to be free of Mexico. The people only wanted to have their own rules to meet their needs. David wrote a very good paper explaining this.

In 1834 Burnet was made the judge of the Department of Brazos. He went to the Consultation and the Convention of 1836. It was there that David Burnet was elected president ad interim of Texas. His good friend and neighbor, Lorenzo de Zavala, was the vice-president.

One of David Burnet's friends was Mirabeau Lamar. Burnet made Lamar Secretary of War and later Commander in Chief of the army. When Lamar became president of the Republic, the friends were together again. Burnet was Lamar's vice-president. There was one thing Lamar did that must have made Burnet sad. Lamar wanted to get rid of the Indians. He sent out soldiers to fight them and many Comanches were killed. Burnet hated the bad things the Indians did, but he had known them as friends.

In the last days of 1841, Lamar left office. Once again David Burnet was president. He had hoped to be elected the third president of the Republic, but the people chose Sam Houston. Five years later, when Texas was a State, Burnet served again. He was the Texas Secretary of State, but this was to be his last office. He went back to his farm, but he was not a good farmer. Every year he grew poorer and poorer. When his wife died in 1858, Burnet went to Galveston to live with friends.

Like Sam Houston, Burnet was against Texas' seceding from the Union. His only son marched off to war and was killed. Burnet was heart broken but there was still one more sadness for David. He was elected to the Senate of the United States in 1866, but he was not allowed to serve. Four years later when he was eighty-two, Burnet died in the home of Preston Perry in Galveston.

During his life, David Burnet had many failures and much sadness. Yet for eight months at the time Texas needed him most, he stood tall. He refused to give way to those who would rule by force. He held together the hopes and dreams of a free country. He gave the people of Texas the chance to make a choice.

## Lorenzo de Zavala

Most people speak only one language. Some people in Texas speak two languages. Lorenzo de Zavala (lō-rän-sō dä sä-vä-lä) was a man who spoke seven languages – Spanish, French, German, Italian, Portuguese, Greek, and English. Yet in every language there were certain words that meant more to him than all others. These were the words that meant "freedom."

Lorenzo was born in Spain on October 3, 1788. His parents moved to Merida, Yucatan, when he was a baby but they sent him to school in Spain. Lorenzo had a fine mind and he liked learning. Perhaps it was in Spain he began to get ideas about freedom. When he came home, he saw how little freedom people in Mexico had.

Yucatan, like all of Mexico, belonged to Spain. The Spanish rulers set up government to carry out their orders. Each town had a council and de Zavala was made the secretary of the council of Merida. He began to talk about the rights of people to speak out and to act freely. The Spanish rulers did not want anyone to question their orders. They did not want the people to get ideas of freedom. To keep Lorenzo quiet they put him in prison for three years.

De Zavala was sent to the prison in the castle of San Juan de Ulloa. This only made Lorenzo stronger in his love of freedom, but he did not waste time being angry. During the long months in prison, Lorenzo studied medicine and English. He could at least learn to help poor, sick people. When he got out of prison, de Zavala went back to Merida as a doctor.

Lorenzo liked helping the sick, but he knew he could do more for people by working with the government. In spite of having been in prison, Lorenzo was elected to the Yucatan Assembly. A year later he went to the Spanish Court in Madrid, Spain, as a representative for Yucatan. The people knew he was smart and they trusted him.

Lorenzo was in Madrid when Mexico declared her independence. He hurried home and was a member of the Mexican Congress from 1822 to 1826. Lorenzo became the president of a meeting to draw up the Constitution of Mexico. This was the Constitution of 1824 which was much like that of the United States. It had a president, congress, and state governments. Lorenzo wanted the states of Mexico to be strong. Others thought all the power should be in the president and congress. Lorenzo was proud that many of his ideas of freedom were a part of the Constitution. He was the first person to sign it.

In 1827 de Zavala became the governor of the State of Mexico. Mexico still was divided on the question of where the power of government should be – with the president or the people. When the new president was chosen, Santa Anna fought to keep power with the people. So did Lorenzo. This was the first of many times the two men were to meet. Lorenzo became the Minister of the Treasury under the second president. Santa Anna was made the highest general in the army. Two years later the government changed again and Lorenzo was put out of office.

It was hard to tell when de Zavala first became interested in Texas. He may have met some of the men who came to Congress asking for land grants in Texas. He asked for a grant himself and got it on March 12, 1829. His grant went from the Sabine River to Nacogdoches, then south to the Gulf of Mexico. He hoped to settle five hundred families on it. Perhaps that is why he took a trip to the United States. When he came back in 1830, he let the Galveston Bay and Texas Land Company take it over.

In 1832 de Zavala was again elected governor of the State of Mexico. By that time Santa Anna had won other battles and was a great hero. He also got rid of the government of President Bustamante who was a dictator. It is not surprising that the people of Mexico wanted Santa Anna for their president. They thought he was really for them.

De Zavala also thought Santa Anna was for the people. He helped Santa Anna get elected and Lorenzo was made a member of the Mexican Chamber of Deputies. It was then that de Zavala began to see that Santa Anna really wanted to be a dictator, too. He wanted to do away with the Constitution of 1824.

Santa Anna did not want de Zavala to make trouble for him. He sent Lorenzo to France as the Minister for Mexico. He knew Lorenzo would do only what was best for the country. He also thought this would keep de Zavala from talking.

Lorenzo knew what Santa Anna was doing, but he made his own plans. He waited until he got to France. Then de Zavala wrote to Santa Anna giving up his post as minister. He told Santa Anna what he thought of him for telling the people one thing and doing another. From that time on de Zavala and Santa Anna were enemies.

De Zavala decided not to go back to Mexico. He spent a year in Spain and then came to Texas. He bought a home on Buffalo Bayou near his friend David Burnet. Burnet had owned a grant next to de Zavala and had turned his over to the Galveston Bay Company also.

Lorenzo hoped to live a quiet life, but things were happening in Texas. The people of Texas had been happy under the Mexican Constitution of 1824. They were not against belonging to Mexico, but Texas wanted to be a separate state. Trouble started when Mexico passed a law against having slaves. It also would not let any more settlers come from the United States. The Texans wanted these laws changed.

Lorenzo must have been proud to know how the Texans felt about the constitution he had helped write. But de Zavala also knew the men who were running the Mexican government. He had fought for the rights of the people in Mexico. Now he would do all he could for the people of his chosen country – Texas.

When Santa Anna learned that de Zavala was in Texas, he tried to have him taken prisoner. The Mexican soldiers would not take Lorenzo. They knew all he had done for the people of Mexico. The Texans would not give him up either. They knew him as a friend and leader.

In October, 1835, there was a meeting of Texas leaders at San Felipe. De Zavala was sent by the town of Harrisburg. Again on March 1, 1836, Lorenzo went to a meeting at Washington-on-the-Brazos. Every man there knew it was time for action. The next day de Zavala signed the Texas Declaration of Independence. He was proud to be a Texan.

For the next two weeks Lorenzo worked

very hard. He was one of twenty-one men who were asked to write a constitution for Texas. Because he had written one, de Zavala knew a great deal about how it should be done. He also wanted to see that mistakes in the Mexican Constitution were not made again. He wanted Texas to have the best government possible.

Early on March 17, the Convention approved the Constitution and elected officers. They were to serve until the people could vote on the Constitution. David Burnet was elected President ad interim (meaning for a short while) and Lorenzo de Zavala was elected Vice President.

The new Republic of Texas lacked many things. For one, it did not have a flag. De Zavala knew how important a flag is to a country, especially during war time. He thought of Texas as a bright new star among the nations of the world. He had a flag made to carry out his idea. Lorenzo's flag had a large white star in the center of a field of bright blue. Between the five points of the star he placed the letters T-E-X-A-S. It was a beautiful flag but the convention never voted on it. Word had just come of the fall of the Alamo. The government left at once for Harrisburg to start its work.

For the next month, de Zavala did everything he could to set up the Republic. He had more experience in government than any other officer. Then word came that Santa Anna was on his way to Harrisburg. De Zavala knew that Santa Anna wanted to capture him more than all the rest. Lorenzo was not afraid of Santa Anna, but he knew that, without a government, Texas would be lost. He and the others went to Galveston to continue

their work.

For the next few days there was no word. Then came the wonderful news. General Sam Houston and the Texans had defeated Santa Anna and his army at San Jacinto. The war was over! Texas was free!

On April 28, 1836, de Zavala and Santa Anna met again. What do you think went through Santa Anna's mind? Perhaps he was sorry he had sent de Zavala to France rather than putting him in prison. Perhaps he wished he had not tried to capture de Zavala and the Texas government. It must have been hard for the proud dictator to be seen a prisoner by the man who he thought was his worst enemy.

Lorenzo saw more than Santa Anna. He saw the many Texans and Mexicans who had been wounded in the battle. His home was just across Buffalo Bayou. He turned it into a hospital for soldiers from both sides.

The Texas government and Santa Anna had to make a treaty. They ended up making two – one public and one secret. In the first one Santa Anna promised to stop fighting and to send all his soldiers back to Mexico. In the secret treaty, Santa Anna promised to try to get Mexico to accept Texas as a free country.

President Burnet asked de Zavala to go back to Mexico with Santa Anna. Lorenzo was to see that the Mexican government agreed to the treaties. Santa Anna and de Zavala got on the ship to leave, but they never left shore. A large group of soldiers made President Burnet keep Santa Anna prisoner in Texas until the regular government was elected.

On September 5, 1836, the people

of Texas voted on the Constitution. They were very pleased with it. It became the plan for how the Republic of Texas was set up. This must have made de Zavala happy.

That same day the people of Texas elected Sam Houston the first president of the Republic. He and the other officers were to take office on the second Monday in December. Members of Congress met on October 3, and soon after Sam Houston joined them. De Zavala thought it best to let the new leaders take over as soon as possible. To make this easy, Lorenzo resigned on October 17, 1836, followed by David Burnet on October 22.

On that day Sam Houston became the first president of the Republic of Texas.

De Zavala went back to his home on Buffalo Bayou. He must have been happy to see Texas free. He had believed in freedom and worked for it all of his life. He had served Texas well and would be ready again if needed, but that was not to be. On November 15, 1836, Lorenzo died.

Lorenzo de Zavala was a man any country would be proud to own. Three had the right to do so. He had been born in Spain. He had lived most of his life in Mexico. Texas was where he died. Of the three, Lorenzo was most proud of being a Texan. He had chosen it for his own.

# The Battle of San Jacinto

On March 6, 1836, two important things happened in Texas. Early that morning the Alamo fell. One hundred eighty-seven brave men gave their lives for Texas. That same day Sam Houston left Washington-on-the-Brazos for Gonzales. The Texas leaders had made him general of all Texas forces. He was on his way to set up his headquarters.

It took Houston five days to get to Gonzales. During that time he had many things to think about. He had to raise an army to fight Santa Anna. He had to train the men how to fight together. He had to protect the people of Texas from the Indians as well as the enemy. He had to plan how to win from an army many times larger than one he could hope to raise. The future of Texas depended on whether he could do all these things.

Houston felt better when he reached Gonzales. Three hundred seventy-four men were waiting for him! At least that was the beginning of an army. But that same night two Mexicans brought the terrible news of the Alamo. Nearly every family in Gonzales lost someone – a father, a son, a husband. How sad everyone was.

To keep word from spreading, Houston put the Mexicans in jail. He said they were spies. Then Houston sent Deaf Smith, his trusted scout, to San Antonio. On the way, Smith met Mrs. Alma Dickinson. There was no denying her story. She had been at the Alamo and had seen everything. She brought a message to Houston from Santa Anna. He promised to kill every person in Texas fighting against him. Then he said he was going to drive all Americans out of Texas.

The news spread quickly. Men, women, and children began to panic. They grabbed a few things and left their homes. Some had wagons or carts to ride upon. Many had to walk. Some drove cows or other farm animals before them. Men who had come to join Houston went back to help their families. Bad men spread the story so they could steal things that were left behind. To make matters worse, heavy spring rains fell. The roads were deep in mud. Streams and rivers overflowed their banks.

Houston decided to move his army to the Colorado River. The army had only two wagons, two yoke of oxen, and a few poor horses. There was very little food for the men and even less gun powder. Houston sent word for men, horses, and supplies to meet him at Beason's Crossing. Then he left Gonzales at midnight. The sky was bright from the fires made by burning houses. Nothing was left that might help the enemy.

Houston's march was very slow. People leaving their homes needed help. Houston sent some of his men to lead the families to the road which the army followed. He sent others to be sure none were left behind. It took almost two days for the families to cross the river at Burnham's. Then the army marched down the river to Beason's Crossing. Houston waited there for the men and supplies he needed.

Since March 1, the leaders of Texas had been busy forming a republic. They signed the Texas Declaration of Independence on March 2. They wrote a constitution for the Republic of Texas. When they signed it on March 17, they elected officers to serve until all the people could vote. Then the officers left Washington-on-the-Brazos for Harrisburg. They had much work to do. They had to get men and supplies for Houston. They had to look after the country and its people. They knew Houston and the army were the only hope of saving Texas.

With the fall of the Alamo, Santa Anna thought the fighting was all but over. He sent soldiers to San Felipe to burn the town. He sent others to Goliad to join General Urrea. He planned to send others to Nacogdoches to run the settlers out of Texas. He got ready to leave for Mexico.

General Sesma was chosen to go to East Texas. He had about seven hundred soldiers with him. He, like Houston, camped at Beason's Crossing. He was just across the Colorado River from Houston.

Many Texas soldiers thought this would be a good time to strike. They felt sure they could beat the enemy. Then came the second piece of terrible news. Fannin and his men had been defeated and killed! This meant that Houston's army stood alone against all the Mexicans!

Houston knew he had just one chance to win. If he fought now, all the other enemy soldiers would come. He must wait for the right time and place for a big victory. Besides, the men and supplies he needed had not come. There was only one thing to do. He had to retreat!

That same night Houston started for San Felipe. When the army reached the Brazos River, some of the men wanted to go down stream. Instead, Houston went up the river toward Groce's Ferry. He marched his men to the Brazos bottom land through heavy spring rains. The flooding river made an island of Houston's camp ground.

For two weeks Houston drilled his men. The supplies came at last. Houston also got two small cannons. They were sent by the people of Cincinnati, Ohio. The men called the cannons the "Twin Sisters."

Houston got word of the enemy from his scouts. General Sesma had crossed the Colorado River with all his men. Santa Anna changed his mind about leaving for Mexico. Instead he set out for Gonzales on March 31. From there he hurried to meet General Sesma at San Felipe.

Houston sent Captain Mosely Baker to San Felipe at once. His orders were to keep Santa Anna from crossing the Brazos there. When Santa Anna could not cross at San Felipe, he went to Fort Bend. From there he marched to Harrisburg where the Texas government was meeting.

Houston sent word for all men to meet at Donoho's on April 16. Donoho's was three miles from Groce's where two roads crossed. One went to Harrisburg. The other went to East Texas.

Many people thought Houston was running away from Santa Anna. They forgot that he was helping women and children get to safety. They did not know how much training the soldiers needed to fight. They did not know what his plans were and why. Even some of the soldiers wondered which road he would take. A great cheer went up when Houston took the road to Harrisburg.

Santa Anna reached Harrisburg on April 15. He wanted to capture the officers of the Texas Republic. He especially wanted to take Lorenzo De Zavala (lō-rāń-sō dā sä-vä-lä). De Zavala had been against Santa Anna in Mexico. Now he was the vice president of the Republic of Texas!

When Santa Anna reached Harrisburg, the Texas leaders had left for Morgan's Point. Santa Anna burned Harrisburg to the ground and then hurried across Buffalo Bayou. By the time he reached Morgan's Point, the Texas leaders had gone to Galveston Island. Santa Anna turned back toward Lynch's Ferry.

Through his scouts, Houston learned that Santa Anna was at Harrisburg. The soldiers were excited. They knew the battle would soon begin. In less than three days the army marched more than fifty miles. The roads were very bad but that did not matter. One day Houston and the soldiers pushed the wagons through the mud eight times.

At Harrisburg, Houston learned that Santa Anna had crossed Buffalo Bayou. This was the chance Houston had hoped for. Houston was no longer in retreat. Santa Anna was in front of him on the south side of Buffalo Bayou. Now Houston could choose where he would fight.

Santa Anna had about seven hundred men with him. Houston had about twelve hundred but many were sick with measles. Houston left about three hundred men at Harrisburg. With the rest of his soldiers, the cavalry, and one wagon with guns and supplies, he crossed the bayou.

On April 20, Houston and his men came to Lynch's Ferry. They captured a boat with food and supplies meant for Santa Anna. Deaf Smith brought word that Santa Anna was only a few miles away. Houston set up camp in some woods along the banks of the bayou and waited. He did not have long to wait.

Santa Anna learned that Houston

and his men were camped in the woods. He tried to draw them into battle. The Mexicans fired their cannons, but they did no damage. Then Santa Anna sent out soldiers into some woods four hundred yards in front of the Texas camp. Houston's cavalry rode out but no fighting happened. Then Houston aimed the "Twin Sisters" on the enemy. This drove them back. Santa Anna then made camp near the bank of the San Jacinto River about a mile away.

The next morning Sam Houston sent for two axes. They were put in a special place. Then he called for Deaf Smith. He told Deaf Smith not to go away from the camp. He had a special job for him.

During the night General Cos and many soldiers crossed Vince's Bridge. They had come to join Santa Anna. Houston told his troops that Santa Anna had marched his men around to try to fool the Texans. Houston did not want his men to lose their high spirits.

About noon General Houston called his officers together. He wanted them to say whether the Texans should attack or wait to be attacked. They did not agree which would be better. General Houston did not say what he thought.

Houston then sent for Deaf Smith. He gave him the two axes and told him to go with a helper to Vince's Bridge to burn it. With this done, no more Mexican soldiers could reach Santa Anna. It also meant no Texans could get away.

About three o'clock in the afternoon, Houston called his men together. The men were ready to fight and they listened well to Houston's battle plan. Houston placed the cavalry at the end of the battle line. Between the cavalry Houston put the soldiers. The "Twin Sisters" were at the very center of the line. Houston told the soldiers not to fire until they came within pistol shot of the enemy.

Houston wanted music to keep the men's spirits high. No one knew a battle

march. Instead the piper and drummer played a song of the day. It was called "Will You Come to the Bower?" It was not the music that made the Texans want to fight. It was cries of, "Remember the Alamo! Remember Goliad!" that made the Texans rush forward. Sam Houston, sitting on his white horse with his sword raised high, led them into battle.

The Mexicans were taken by surprise. Santa Anna did not think Houston would dare attack him. He had put few look-outs in the camp. This was a time of siesta. Many of the men were sleeping. Some were playing cards. Others were cooking. The Texans were upon them before they knew what was happening. And what a fight it was!

The Texans fought like wild men. The Mexican soldiers were used to fighting in rows. They acted on orders from their officers. The officers had no time to get the men in line. Besides, the guns were stacked in great piles.

In eighteen minutes the battle was over. Those who were not killed ran away as fast as they could. Some Mexicans jumped into the river. Others ran into the swamp. A few tried to get to Vince's Bridge. No matter where they went, the Texans were right behind them. In the end 630 Mexicans were killed and 208 of the 730 prisoners were wounded. Only nine of the 910 Texans were killed and thirty wounded. General Houston was one of the wounded.

General Santa Anna could not be found among the dead or the prisoners.

Had he gotten away? It was too dark to look for him that night, but the search went on the next morning.

During the day some Texans came upon a soldier dressed like a common private. He had a blanket over his head and acted as if he were dead. The Texans were not fooled. They brought him back to camp. As he passed the Mexicans, they bowed to the prisoner. The Texans knew he was someone important so they brought him to General Houston. It was Santa Anna.

Houston was seated under an oak tree. He had been shot in the ankle and was in much pain. He might have been very hard on Santa Anna. Many Texans wanted to kill him at once, but Houston greeted him politely.

Santa Anna wanted to deal with General Houston to get free. General Houston would not do this. He told Santa Anna he would have to deal with the leaders of the Republic of Texas. Houston did make Santa Anna write to his generals. Santa Anna ordered them with all their soldiers to leave Texas. He also told them not to hurt any Texans. Houston sent Deaf Smith with these letters to be sure they reached the Mexican generals.

April 22, 1836, was the first free day in Texas. The fighting was over and Texas had won. This did not mean all the trouble was over. The people of Texas had to learn how to rule themselves. They had to deal with all the problems of a new nation, but this was a good beginning for the Republic of Texas.

# Sam Houston, Hero of San Jacinto

Do you have a special ring? Many people do. Sometimes a ring is special because of the person who gave it to you. Maybe you like your ring because it shows you belong to a club or class. Some people like a ring because of the pretty stones on it. Sam Houston had a special ring. It was a plain band of gold. Inside was written one word, HONOR.

On the day before he was twenty years old, Sam's mother gave him the ring. Sam wanted to join the army, but he had to have her permission. Mrs. Houston put the ring on Sam's finger. She told him to wear it forever. Honor was to be the first rule of his life. Sam promised to live by this rule.

For many people, joining the army is their first big adventure. This was not true of Sam Houston. He was born on a plantation in Virginia on March 2, 1793. Sam and his eight brothers and sisters had a good life. Sam went to school and learned reading and writing but not much math.

When Sam was thirteen, things changed. His father died and the family moved to Maryville, Tennessee. Everyone had to work to clear the land for their home and fields. Sam wanted neither to work nor to study. He loved to read, especially Greek and Roman history. Often he slipped away to the woods. This made his family unhappy, for everyone had to do his part. Mrs. Houston sent Sam to work in a store. Sam did not like this very much either. When he was sixteen he left home.

For most of the next three years Sam lived with the Cherokee Indians. He lived in the village of Chief Oolooteka. He was a wise chief who lived at peace with the white settlers. Oolooteka means "he-puts-the-drum-away." Sam learned the ways of the Cherokees. He spoke their language and understood how they felt about man and nature. Sam dressed like an Indian and he became a member of the tribe. To Chief Oolooteka Houston became a son. He was given the name Colonneh which means "rover." Houston always said it meant "the Raven." Both names suited him.

Sam came back to Maryville only to buy presents for his Indian friends. The third time, he found that he owed one hundred dollars for his last gifts. To earn the money, Houston opened a school! It ran from May to November and cost each pupil eight dollars. When Houston's school was over, he knew he needed to go to school himself. He went to Porter Academy (for a few months) until he joined the army on March 1, 1813.

Sam was a fine looking man. He stood over six feet tall. He had fair skin, blue eyes and reddish hair. As a soldier, he stood out from the rest of the privates. He had the look of a leader and proved to be one. In the Battle of Horseshoe Bend, Houston was wounded, but he fought on. General Andrew Jackson promoted him on the spot for his bravery. This was the beginning of a life long friendship between these men.

Houston was in the army for five years. He was made agent to Chief Oolooteka's band of Cherokees. Houston's job was to get the Cherokees to move to Arkansas. Then Houston went to Washington with another band of Cherokees. Houston dressed as an Indian so he might speak as one of them. He wore a blanket and a buckskin coat. There were metal objects

on the coat that tinkled as he walked. This was not the dress of an army officer, but Houston liked it. The Secretary of War did not! Things were said that seemed to question Houston's honor. Houston was deeply hurt. He left the army.

Houston decided to go to Nashville, Tennessee. He studied law and in six months passed the bar. He was a good lawyer and made money and friends. He became adjutant general of the state militia. As its colonel and later major general, Houston traveled all over Tennessee. Houston was also elected attorney general of Davidson County. He worked hard, but he found time for fun. He went to many parties and balls.

Houston first became interested in Texas in 1822. By then, Mexico was letting settlers come to Texas. Houston asked the Mexican government for grants of land. He saw this as a way to make money. Nothing ever came of this, but other things were happening to Houston. He was elected to Congress! He served in 1823 and again in 1825. In 1827 Houston became Governor of Tennessee. Some people thought he might be president one day.

On January 1, 1829, Houston and Eliza Allen were married. The bride was of a fine family. She was blond, very beautiful, and tiny. Houston was tall and handsome but he was twice her age. It seemed that Houston had everything, but this was not to be. Eliza went home to her parents by the middle of April. Houston never told what the trouble was, but he resigned as governor. Then he left Nashville for Arkansas. He was on his way back to join the Cherokees.

For the next six years Houston lived with the Indians. He was very sad and he felt sorry for himself. He started drinking a great deal. Some of the Indians called him "Big Drunk," yet there were times when he helped them. He went to Washington to get what was due them from the government. He ran a trading post called the Wigwam. He also married Tiana Rogers. Chief Oolooteka was her uncle and her brothers were Houston's friends. Sam Houston became a Cherokee citizen.

The first trip Houston made to Texas was in December, 1832. He came for two reasons. He wanted to make peace between the Comanches and the Cherokees. He also was to let Andrew Jackson know about the Indians in Texas. Houston went to Nacogdoches on the way to San Felipe. He asked for a grant of land. He said he wanted to settle it himself. He spent Christmas in San Felipe with Jim Bowie. Bowie went with him to San Antonio to meet the Comanches. On Houston's way back, the people of Nacogdoches asked him to return in April. They wanted him to go to the Convention for them. He did but it was two years before Houston came to Texas to live.

In 1835 there was a restless spirit in Texas. Many people wanted to be a part of Mexico. They only wanted Texas to be a separate state. Others wanted Texas to be free. Everything that happened brought war a step closer.

The people in Nacogdoches made Houston Commander in Chief of volunteers in that area. They also sent him to the third Convention which set up a Provisional Government. The Convention made Houston Commander in Chief of the Texas army. There were two things wrong with this. Houston had to obey both the President and the Council. Then there was no real army, only volunteers who came and went as they pleased.

For one month Houston stayed in San Felipe with the government. He had to make plans to get, train, and keep an army. He had to order uniforms, food, and supplies. He had to get money from the government to pay soldiers and buy things. He was getting ready for the war that was coming.

Many Texans were already fighting. They were camped near San Antonio. General Cos and his soldiers were in the city. On December 5, Ben Milam led the attack and six days later General Cos gave up. Many Texans thought this was the end of fighting. They left to go home but some of the men had other plans. They wanted to march to Matamoros and fight in Mexico.

By this time the President and the Council were fighting. What one wanted, the other did not. The Council thought marching on Matamoros was a good plan. The President and Sam Houston did not. The Council made Colonel Fannin an agent to raise money and men for this attack. The Council also told Colonel Johnson to go to Matamoros. Colonel Johnson took most of the men from the Alamo with him.

On January 8, 1836, Houston left his headquarters for Goliad. He had sent orders that the march should not begin until he got there. When Houston met Colonel Johnson, he showed Houston a paper from the Council. It gave Johnson and Fannin power to act without permission from Houston. It made them more powerful than the Commander in Chief.

Houston returned at once to Washington-on-the-Brazos. He made a report to Governor Smith. Then he asked for leave until March 1. He went to the Cherokees to make sure they would not fight against the Texans.

Houston returned to Washington-on-the-Brazos on March 1. The next day he was one of the fifty-nine persons who signed the Texas Declaration of Independence. On March 4, Houston was made Commander in Chief of all forces in Texas. This time he really was in command.

Houston left Washington for Gonzales on March 6. By the eleventh he learned of the fall of the Alamo. He was met by three hundred seventy-four men. They were volunteers, not trained soldiers. In spite of his plans, Houston had no uniforms, guns, nor supplies for them. He had no money to pay them. The enemy he faced had everything he lacked. There were at least seven thousand trained enemy soldiers in Texas.

For the next month Houston marched his men toward the East. He needed time. He hoped to get more men as he went along, but they needed to be trained. He had to wait for guns and supplies before he could fight. He knew the farther he drew the enemy from their supplies, the better his chance of winning. But to many Texans, it looked as if Houston were running away.

Santa Anna really thought the fighting was over at the Alamo. However, he wanted to drive all Americans out of Texas. He divided his troops so they might spread across the land. He started with about seven hundred men for Harrisburg. That was where the Texas government was meeting.

When Houston learned that Santa Anna had gone to Harrisburg, he started there at once. He knew his only chance of winning was to defeat Santa Anna. Santa Anna had gone to Morgan's Point. He wanted to capture the Texas govern-

ment before it could get to Galveston. When he missed them, Santa Anna came back toward Lynch's Ferry. Houston was waiting for him. On April 21, at siesta time in the afternoon, Houston attacked. In eighteen minutes it was all over. The Texans had won the Battle of San Jacinto!

During the battle, Houston had three horses shot from under him. He also was wounded in the ankle. He would not leave until Santa Anna had been turned over to the Texas government. On May 5, Houston went to New Orleans to have his ankle treated. The wound never healed, but Houston came back to Texas in June.

On September 5, 1836, the people of Texas voted on the Constitution. They also elected officers of the new Republic of Texas. Houston, the hero of the Battle of San Jacinto, was chosen the first President. On October 22, at 4:00 o'clock p.m., under a large live oak tree in Columbia, Houston took the oath of office.

Houston had two main problems to deal with first. He needed to see that Santa Anna got back to Mexico safely. Mexico must agree to the treaty Santa Anna had signed. Houston also knew that the United States must accept the Texas Republic as a free country. The Texans had voted to join the United States, but it would be ten years before this happened.

Houston had many other things to do and only two years in which to do them. He had to set up the government and find ways in which to pay for it. He started courts and a post office. He divided the country into counties and laid out public lands. He needed to make the Republic known among the other nations of the world.

It was a busy two years. Sometimes Houston had to make things do until a lasting answer could be found. When at first there was no state seal, Houston fixed that. He used one of his cuff links until a seal could be made. The cuff link showed a dog's head, a cock, the letter H, and the words "Try Me."

When Mirabeau Lamar became the second president, Houston showed up dressed like George Washington in white wig and knee britches. Houston spoke for three hours! Perhaps he thought this was proper for the first president. Perhaps he thought this was his last public speech.

Or maybe he was already running for the job again. Yet when Houston became the third president of the Republic, he was dressed very differently. He wore a "linsey-woolsey hunting shirt and pantaloons with an old wide-brimmed white fur hat." Sam Houston really liked clothes!

On May 9, 1840, Houston married Margaret Lea. She was from Alabama. Sam met her at the home of her brother in Mobile. Margaret was very religious and because of her Sam joined the church. They had eight children and were very happy even though Houston spent much time away from home.

When Texas became the twenty-eighth state of the Union, Sam Houston was one of its first senators. For almost fourteen years he served the State well in Washington. On bills dealing with the Indians, Houston spoke for their interest. He also spoke on the need for all states to be loyal to the government. This was the time when slavery was dividing the country. Houston thought that the Union was more important than any of its parts.

In 1857 Houston tried to be governor of Texas again. He knew that some of the Southern States would soon leave the Union. He felt it would be bad for Texas to join them. He thought as governor he could keep this from happening. For the first time in his life, Houston lost, but two years later he became governor.

Houston had not realized how strongly most Texans felt. He spoke against leaving the Union but the people did not agree. When Lincoln became president, many Southern States seceded. The Texas legislature demanded that the people vote on secession. Houston was against this but the date was set.

On February 23, 1861, Texas voted to secede. The date this act was to happen was March 2, twenty-five years after Texas gained her independence. With a sad heart, Houston announced that Texas had seceded. He hoped that Texas would become once again a republic. Instead the people wanted to join the Confederacy.

The Texas Convention voted that all state officers had to support the Confederacy. Houston could not do what he thought was wrong. He had to be true to his sense of honor. All the state officers came together to take an oath of loyalty. When Houston's name was called, there was no answer. Houston was in his office. His name was called a second time.

Again there was no answer. Edward Clark became governor of Texas.

Houston and his family moved to Huntsville. Before long Texas was sending men to fight in the War between the States. Houston's oldest son joined the army and was wounded. It was a sad time for old Sam.

Houston, Margaret, and his other children lived quietly in Huntsville. In July, 1863, Houston became ill. The news from the battle front made him sad. As the month passed, Houston grew weaker. On July 26, Houston died. Margaret took the plain gold band off her husband's finger. It had been there for fifty years. Inside, the one word "Honor" was as bright as the day on which the ring was put on.

The editor of the *Telegraph* wrote this about Sam Houston:

"He has not alway been right, nor has he always been successful, but he has always kept the impress of his mind upon the times in which he acted."

## *Mirabeau Buonaparte Lamar*

It was late in the afternoon of April 20, 1836. The Texas army under General Sam Houston was camped along the bank of Buffalo Bayou. About a mile away General Santa Anna and his army were setting up their camp. It was too late to begin a battle, but the Texans were restless. The cavalry wanted to test the enemy so General Houston agreed to let the horsemen scout the enemy's camp.

As the Texans drew near, the Mexican cavalry rode out to meet them. Thomas J. Rusk, the Texas Secretary of War, was with the cavalry. In the clash between the two groups, Rusk and another man were cut off from the Texans. Suddenly a Texas rider left his company, attacked the Mexicans around Rusk, drove the enemy back and rescued the Texans. The rider then rode back to his company in full view of the enemy soldiers. The Mexicans fired a salute to the brave rider who stopped his horse and bowed to the soldiers.

The Mexicans were not the only ones who saw this brave act. When the cavalry got back to camp, General Houston called the rider to him. The man was Mirabeau Lamar, a private with the army less than a month. Houston made Lamar a colonel and the next day he led the cavalry in the Battle of San Jacinto.

Lamar was a man of many talents and broad experience. As a boy in Georgia he became a fine horseman and fencer. He loved to read and he wrote well, especially poems. He also liked to paint with oil paint. As a young man he ran a store and edited a newspaper in Alabama. He was secretary to the governor of Georgia and also served in the legislature. Later he started the *Enquirer* newspaper in Columbus, Georgia.

Not all of Lamar's life in Georgia was happy. His beautiful young wife died and left him with a baby girl to look after. He ran for Congress in 1832 and again in 1834 but lost both times. His health became poor and he came to Texas in 1835 to try to get well. He liked the country so much he went back to Georgia to sell his newspaper. While he was there he heard about the Alamo and Goliad. Lamar hurried back just in time to fight at San Jacinto.

When Sam Houston went to New Orleans to have his wound treated, Thomas Rusk became general of the army. This left the office of Secretary of War empty. President David Burnet had heard of Lamar's bravery and he liked him. The President made Lamar Secretary of War. As Secretary, Lamar wanted Santa Anna killed for his acts against Texas, but the government would not do it.

About a month later President Burnet made Lamar commander in chief of the Texas army. Lamar was very pleased but the army was not. The soldiers felt that General Houston was still their commander. Lamar had been brave at San Jacinto, but he had no experience as an army leader. Lamar could do nothing to change their minds. He left the government and went to Brazoria to live.

Lamar was interested in the history of Texas. He began to try to learn more about it so he could write a book. Brazoria was a place where many early settlers lived and where Jane Long ran her boardinghouse. Lamar, like many other people, found Jane a good friend. He wrote poems to her and would have liked to marry her, but that never happened.

In September, 1836, the people of Texas voted on its constitution and elected officers. Sam Houston became the first president of the Republic and Lamar the vice president. As vice president, Lamar was in charge of the meetings of the Senate. Since the Senate did not meet all the time, Lamar went back to Georgia. He wanted to see his little girl and finish his business there. He also wanted to tell others about Texas.

While Lamar was in Georgia, his friends in Texas decided he should be the next president. Two other men wanted the office but both killed themselves before the election. Lamar won by almost every vote.

On December 10, 1838, Lamar became the second president of the Texas Republic. Lamar had big plans. He felt that Texas should cover all the land between the Sabine River and the Pacific Ocean. He thought this would bring riches and power to the Republic. He also wanted to set up schools and colleges. He knew that a great country needed men and women with trained minds and broad learning. These were great dreams, but dreams need action to become real.

Before Lamar could work on his dreams, he had to face a number of problems. There was no money in the State treasury. Texas still had debts from the battles with Mexico and she had little to trade. The Indians were angry with the settlers who moved onto their lands and they were ready to fight. The Mexicans also wanted to march against the Texans and capture the land again. Only the United States had accepted Texas as a free republic. None of the other countries of the world would do so.

Lamar tried to make friends with England, France, and Holland. He hoped to set up trade with them to raise money. He also wanted their help in getting Mexico to accept Texas as a republic.

As for the Indians, Lamar took a hard stand. Where Sam Houston had tried to be friends with the Indians, Lamar sent soldiers to fight them. He wanted to drive the Indians out of Texas once and for all.

Like all presidents, Lamar had bills he wanted passed by Congress. One was the Homestead Act. It was like the bill Stephen Austin had passed for the settlers. It kept anyone from taking someone's home to pay for debts. Each home owner could keep his house, his tools, fifty acres of land and his furniture. To be sure the home owner could live to pay his debts, the law also let him keep five milk cows, one yoke of oxen or one horse, twenty hogs, and one year's supply of food.

Lamar was most proud of one law – the Education Act. When Texas was part of Mexico there were no free public schools. The people asked the government to set up schools but Mexico did not do it. This became one reason Texas broke with Mexico. The people knew how much their children needed to learn. In some towns they tried to start schools themselves, but many children never had a chance to go. Whenever people could find someone to teach, they would ask them to start a school. Often the teacher could hardly read and write himself. There were no textbooks so children brought any book for a reader.

Lamar got the Texas Congress to set aside three leagues of land in each county. This was 13,248 acres for schools in each county. He also had fifty leagues set aside for two universities. In 1840 Congress gave another league in each county to buy desks and supplies for schools. It was many years before free public schools opened and the two universities were built, but Lamar is known as the "Father of Education."

The city of Houston was the capital of Texas when Lamar became president. Lamar thought the capital should be nearer the center of the country. He had gone hunting near a town called Waterloo on the west bank of the Colorado River. Lamar thought it would be the perfect place for the capital. In November, 1839, Congress met for the first time in this new capital named for Stephen F. Austin.

Lamar was very pleased with the new capital. He saw it as the center of an empire stretching to the Pacific Ocean. He wanted Texas to take in New Mexico, Arizona, Nevada, California, Oregon, and Washington. Texas claimed all that land even though Mexico had never agreed that Texas was a free country.

Lamar had a plan for building his empire. He knew that the people of New Mexico did not like being a part of Mexico. He also knew that Santa Fe was a town where much trading went on. Because Texas was having money troubles, Lamar thought taking Santa Fe would be a first step toward his dream.

Lamar asked Congress for money to send soldiers to Santa Fe. Congress did not think this was a good plan nor did it have the money to pay for it. Lamar did get Congress to agree to let some soldiers and other men make the trip. On June 21, 1841, a group of 270 soldiers and fifty other men left Austin for Santa Fe.

From the very first, things went wrong with the Santa Fe Expedition. There were not enough supplies and the guides were not sure of the way. It was about one thousand miles from Austin to Santa

Fe, but the group marched almost thirteen hundred miles. There were days when the men were hungry and thirsty. They burned up during the day and froze at night.

At the end of three months the men were worn out by all the hardships. They still had not reached Santa Fe, but the people there had word of the Expedition. Santa Fe might not like the Mexicans, but the people did not want to belong to Texas! They sent Mexican soldiers to look for the Texans. The Mexicans captured the Texans and marched them off to prison in Mexico. Lamar's dream of an empire was over.

The Santa Fe Expedition became a sad ending to Lamar's days as president. Texas now had debts ten times bigger than when he had taken office. Mexico was still an enemy. The United States still had not agreed to let Texas become a state. Many unkind things were said about Lamar, who most people thought was a "wild dreamer."

With the election of Sam Houston as president, Lamar went to Richmond to live. He was a neighbor of Jane Long's again and he spent his days writing the history of Texas. He decided he would not have anything more to do with Texas government.

In 1843 Lamar's daughter died. Whenever a great sadness came to him, he always took a trip. This time Lamar went to Mobile, Alabama; New York City; and Washington, D.C. As president, Lamar had not wanted Texas to join the Union. Now he thought this would be best for Texas, so he spoke about it to people in Washington.

When the United States and Mexico went to war, Lamar joined the army. He became a lieutenant colonel and later was in charge of soldiers guarding the Rio Grande border. In spite of his earlier word, Lamar helped set up the government for the town of Laredo. He also went to the state legislature in 1847.

In 1851 Lamar married again. He and his bride lived happily near Richmond although he seemed always in debt. In 1856 Lamar left for Nicaragua and Costa Rica. He was the United States minister to these countries. Once more Lamar saw the great need for schools for the people. He could not make those countries set up schools, but he did something else. He gave two hundred books to start the Nicaragua National Library.

Lamar came home in 1859. He was happy to be with his family again. As earlier, he wrote a great deal. He had traveled and had many experiences to share through his writings. It was perhaps the best time of his life. Then he died quite suddenly on December 19, 1859.

Many things were said about Lamar. No one could doubt that he was brave. Some saw him as foolish because of the Santa Fe Expedition. Others thought he was a poor leader because of the heavy debts he put on Texas. Yet for one thing, Lamar should always be given honor. He knew how important learning was for every person and each nation. Because of his dreams and his work, Texas has great universities and public schools today.

# Anson Jones

In October, 1833, a ship from New Orleans landed at the town of Brazoria, Texas. Most of the people who got off were excited. This was their first sight of the land they had chosen for their homes. It looked good to them for their minds were fixed on the future life they hoped to make for their families.

One man did not share the feelings of the crowd. He stood aside while the others hurried to get ashore. What he saw was a muddy road and a row of wooden buildings that were gray from the wind and weather. How different it was from the city of New Orleans where he had lived for a year! The thought of New Orleans made him feel bad, for it was the last place where he had been a failure. It seemed everything he had ever tried to do was a failure.

The man found the ship's captain who was watching the sailors unload the settler's belongings. The ship had other supplies to take to Copano, but it would come back to Brazoria before returning to New Orleans. The man paid the captain to take him back to New Orleans when the ship returned. This left him with seventeen dollars. That was all the money he had in the world.

At last the man picked up his two bags and walked down the muddy road to a rooming house. One bag held his clothes. The other was a doctor's bag. Although he had not practiced medicine for a year, he could not bring himself to get rid of the bag.

For a few days until the ship returned, the man spent most of the time alone. He spoke very little and did not try to make friends. Most of the settlers left Brazoria as quickly as possible and soon the lonely man was the only stranger in town.

The people who lived in Brazoria were

always interested in strangers. The settlers got news of the world from strangers and many times they became friends. People at the rooming house had seen the two bags the man had brought. They knew his name was Jones, Anson Jones, but they knew very little else about him. Was he really a doctor? That would be good news, because they needed a doctor very badly.

The people of Brazoria got together and asked John Wharton to talk to Jones to find out about him. Jones told Wharton that he had first been licensed as a doctor in New York in 1820, but that he later had recieved a degree from Jefferson Medical College in Philadelphia. He probably did not tell Wharton that he had never had a good practice nor that the drug store and other businesses he had tried had all failed. Even if he had, that would not have mattered. The people of Brazoria needed a doctor and Wharton begged Jones to "give Texas a fair trial." Jones had nothing else to do so he agreed.

Staying in Texas was the best thing Anson Jones had ever done. At the end of one year he had made five thousand dollars as a doctor. That was a lot of money in those days. He was still very quiet, but many people found out how smart he was.

As Jones learned more about Texas, he at first wanted to keep peace with Mexico, but in 1835 he changed his mind. He signed a paper asking people in each town to send someone to a meeting called the Consultation. Jones hoped Texas would declare her independence, but instead the people said they wanted to live by the Mexican Constitution of 1824.

They did say that they wanted to become a separate state of Mexico.

When the war with Mexico started, Jones joined the army as a plain soldier. When General Houston was training his army near Groce's Point, many men became sick. Colonel Sidney Sherman begged Jones to become the doctor for his soldiers. Jones really wanted to fight, but he agreed to look after the men if Sherman would let him fight as a regular soldier. Jones proved what a good doctor he was because not a single man under Sherman's orders died.

When General Houston crossed Buffalo Bayou on the way to San Jacinto, he left the soldiers who were sick in Harrisburg. Anson Jones looked after his sick soldiers first and then he crossed the Bayou. He fought bravely in the Battle of San Jacinto but he spent the night of April 21 and the next day treating the wounded. On the battlefield he found a book written by Juan Almonte, the aide to Santa Anna. This was the record of the war as the Mexicans saw it. Jones sent the book to a newspaper in New York where it was printed in 1836.

When General Houston took Santa Anna to Galveston to make a treaty with the Texas government, Jones went with them. Anson became the Assistant Surgeon General of the army and went to New Orleans to get medical supplies. He went back to Brazoria when he got out of the army.

Jones was a man who did not push himself or his ideas on people, but he was not a man to be pushed around. When he reached Brazoria, he found that James Collinsworth had taken over his office and refused to get out. Jones dared him to meet in a duel with "pistols at ten steps." When Collinsworth found out that Jones meant to go through with the duel, Collinsworth left the office.

After Texas became a republic, Jones became interested in its government. He knew that the acts of its congress would decide whether Texas would become a strong nation or a weak one. He was elected to the Second Congress and helped pass a number of good laws. He wanted to set up schools and a university, but his most important work was as head of the Committee on Foreign Relations. Although most people wanted Texas to become part of the United States at once, he thought the Republic should prove itself first.

Jones planned to marry Mrs. Mary McCrory when his term in the Texas Congress was over, but President Sam Houston changed those plans. He asked Jones to go to the United States as the minister from the Republic. Since the United States had not shown any interest in letting Texas become a state, Jones was to let it be known that Texas no longer was asking for this. Instead Jones tried to get countries in Europe to accept Texas as a republic and to begin trade with Texas. If this happened, Texas would become strong enough to stand as a free nation. It would also make the United States more interested in annexing Texas. Because of this plan, Jones was called the "Architect of Annexation."

Soon after Mirabeau Lamar became the second president of the Republic, he made someone else the minister to Washington. Jones hoped to go back to Brazoria and get married, but he had been chosen a senator in the Texas Con-

gress. Again he was made the head of the Committee on Foreign Affairs.

At last Jones married Mrs. McCrory in May, 1840. Anson and his bride went back to Brazoria, but when Houston was elected president again, he made Jones his Secretary of State. From December 13, 1841, until February 16, 1846, Jones was in charge of all matters dealing with foreign countries.

In all the years since the Battle of San Jacinto, Mexico had never agreed that Texas was a free nation. Houston and Jones both wanted this to happen. At the same time they wanted the United States to ask Texas to join with all its other states. If both things happened together, the people of Texas would be able to choose which way would be best for them and for Texas – independence as a nation or becoming a state.

Jones ran for president in 1844, but it was not the way most people would do it. He did not make a single speech! Maybe that is the reason people elected him. By then the United States had decided it wanted to annex Texas. The people of Texas wanted to know whether Jones was for joining the United States or not, but Anson would not say. He was still hoping to get Mexico to sign a peace treaty and agree that Texas was a free country. Both France and England promised to help him with Mexico, but there was no one to help him with Texas. The people were angry because he did not take the offer from the United States at once. They wanted to throw him out of office and they even burned a straw man they called "Anson Jones" to show how angry they were.

On June 4, 1845, Jones got the treaty

from Mexico that agreed to peace between the countries. As president, Anson brought the treaty before the Texas Congress to have the paper signed, but Congress would not do so. Congress wanted to join the United States. Jones then called a convention to write a state constitution for the United States to see. If it met all requirements, Texas could become a state.

On December 29, 1845, the President of the United States signed the paper to make Texas the twenty-eighth state of the Union. It was February 19, 1846, when the officers of the Republic of Texas gave place to those of the State of Texas. J. Pinkney Henderson was the first Texas governor, but Anson Jones is the one who is remembered on that day. Jones marked the passing of a great period of history when he said, "The final act in this great drama is now performed. The Republic of Texas is no more!" As Jones lowered the national flag, the staff broke in two.

That same day marked the end of Jones' public life in Texas. He really wanted to be made a senator from Texas, but Houston and Thomas J. Rusk were chosen by the legislature. Jones did not get a single vote. Then Jones went to his new home, Barrington, where he bought much land and became rich. For a man who came to Texas with only seventeen dollars, Anson had become a big success, but he was not happy.

In 1849 Jones had a chance to be elected to the United States Congress, but he would not take it. He thought he should be a senator. That same year, he fell from a horse and hurt his left arm so badly that he was always in pain. He could not use his left hand and wore a black glove on it.

Jones wrote a book called *The Republic of Texas* that has many important papers and letters from his time in government. It is a book that helps people understand what happened, but it may have been bad for Anson. He remembered the anger of the people during the last months he was president. He thought about how bad he felt when the legislature would not even thank him for all he had done. He could not forget the things he had wanted that others had obtained. Anson became more and more unhappy.

In November, 1858, Jones believed that he would at last become a senator from Texas, taking the place of Sam Houston, but one more time the Texas legislature passed over Jones. He did not get a single vote. The blow was more than he could stand.

In January, Jones left his family in Galveston and went to Houston. He took a room in the Old Capitol Hotel where he had stayed many times on government business. This time he was there for a different reason. On the morning of January 9, 1859, Jones was found dead in his room. He had taken his own life.

Just as when he first came to Texas, Anson Jones looked back on his life and saw only his failures. Yet Anson Jones should be remembered for all the good things he did. Without his hard work, the people of Texas might never have had the chance to choose their way to the future.

## The Texas Rangers

Stephen F. Austin faced many problems when he became the first Texas empresario. He had to choose the land where people would want to build homes and raise crops. He had to choose the people who would make good settlers and obey the laws of Mexico. He had to help them get started in their new life, but there was one thing he could not do alone. He could not protect the settlers from the Indians.

In 1823 Austin sent out a call for men to fight the Indians. They would have to be brave men, willing to risk their lives to save the settlers. They would have to be without any fear. Austin chose ten men who came up to these requirements and they became the first Rangers. Three years later there were about twenty Rangers.

From the first, Rangers were special people. Each man rode his own horse, brought his own gun, and carried the food and other things he needed. Each man had to be able to cook and look after himself and his horse. Any man who became the leader of the Rangers did so because he had won the respect of all the others.

There was no way of telling where or when the Indians might strike the settlers. They would appear suddenly, do whatever they pleased, and dash away into the wild country. Once the news of the attack came to the Rangers, they were off to hunt the Indians wherever they might have gone.

After the Indians were trailed to their camp, the Rangers made ready to attack. With their long barreled rifles, they could shoot the Indians from a great distance. However, once the trigger was pulled, there was a time of waiting to fire again.

The Ranger had to put powder and lead shot into the rifle which gave the Indian time to fire his own gun. These fights often lasted a long time, but in the end they were always deadly, sometimes for both sides. The Rangers soon learned never to let themselves be captured. The Indians tortured any man they took and made the death as long and painful as possible.

The Indians soon found out what great fighters the Rangers were, but this did not stop their attacks on the settlers. The settlers knew how much they needed the Rangers, and in 1835 the Provisional Texas Government made them legal. They sent two companies of Rangers to the Brazos and Trinity Rivers. During the Revolution, the Rangers protected the women and children from Indian and Mexican attacks.

When Texas became a republic, she was too poor to keep an army. What she needed was a group of men who could meet any enemy quickly, be it Indian or Mexican. The Rangers were such a group and they had many chances to prove themselves. It was during the Republic that Ben McCulloch, Sam Walker, John McMullen, Addison Gillespie, Big Foot Wallace, and Old Paint Caldwell joined the Rangers. Each was a leader on his own, but they all followed another man named John Coffee Hays. The Rangers called him Jack, but his enemies had other names for him. He was El Diablo, or the devil, to the Mexicans.

There was one way in which the Indians were better than the Rangers. They were both fine horsemen, but the Indians could shoot their arrows while riding their horses at top speed. The Rangers had only rifles which were too long and too heavy to fire while riding. To take good aim, a Ranger had to dismount his horse to shoot and then he had to reload his gun before it could be fired again. If only another gun that was lighter and faster could be found, the enemies would be better matched.

Someone far away had come up with a gun that was just what the Rangers needed. Samuel Colt in Connecticut had invented a gun which would shoot six times before having to be re-loaded. He called it a revolver. He had tried to sell it to the United States Army, but they would not buy it.

In some way, a few of these revolvers reached the Ranger camp outside of San Antonio. Jack Hays and his Rangers were excited about the gun and they tried it out at once on a target. Six shots hit the target very quickly. The Rangers were

delighted. Here was the gun they had been looking for.

The Rangers decided to use the revolver the next time they met their old enemy – the Comanches. They did not have long to wait. The Comanches attacked a settlement near San Antonio and quickly rode away. The Rangers came upon them near the Pedernales River.

Hays told his men to dismount and to fire their rifles as always. As the Indians came near to shoot their arrows among the Rangers, the white men jumped on their horses. They started chasing the Indians, firing their six shooters as they rode. The Indians could not believe what was happening. The chief escaped but it was told that he never wanted to meet the Rangers again. At last the Rangers could fight the Indians on horseback! When Colt heard that the Rangers were

using his gun, he named it Texas.

The Indians were not the only enemy the Rangers had to fight. Mexico would not agree that Texas was a free republic. Instead she thought of Texas as a state that needed to be punished and brought back under Mexican rule. At times small bands of Mexicans crossed into Texas and caused trouble. The Rangers were sent to protect the border.

The Texans could not let such actions go without doing something about them. On two occasions the Rangers captured Laredo to see that trade was not stopped, but it was a big expedition that really angered Mexico. President Lamar sent an expedition to Santa Fe to try to get this town and all of New Mexico to join Texas. The trip was a failure from the beginning and ended with all the Texans being captured. They were all sent to prison, but Mexico decided to teach Texas a lesson.

In March and again in September, 1842, Mexico sent soldiers to capture San Antonio. Neither force stayed long, but General Woll took as prisoners the court which was meeting in San Antonio. The Rangers never were large enough as a group to fight the Mexican troops but they followed the Mexicans to see that they left Texas.

Many of the men who followed the Mexican troops stopped at the border, but others wanted to cross into Mexico. The town of Mier was just across the river and volunteers marched on the town to capture it. Instead the Texans were captured. John Hays and Ben McCulloch did not cross into Mexico, but Sam Walker and Big Foot Wallace did.

The Texas prisoners tried to escape but they were caught and brought back to jail. Santa Anna wanted to kill all of them but decided instead to kill one of every ten men. The question of which ones to kill was decided in a strange way. A jar was placed on a table. Into it were placed 179 beans, 162 were white ones and 17 were black.

Each prisoner drew a bean out of the jar. If he drew a white one, he lived to march to Perote prison. If he drew a black one, he was shot in the sight of all the other Texans. Sam Walker and Big Foot Wallace drew white beans. They were in Perote prison for almost three years.

When Texas became the twenty-eighth state of the United States, Mexico was very angry. She placed her army along the border ready to march into Texas again. This time there was no way this could happen, for the United States placed its army on the other side of the border.

Texas had never seen such a well equipped army, but it lacked one thing. The Americans did not know the country nor the people they were about to fight. They needed help and who could do a better job than the Rangers? Captain Jack Hays was made a colonel and given the job of having his men act as scouts and spies. Hays made the men who had served with him in San Antonio his captains – Ben McCulloch, Sam Walker, Big Foot Wallace, and others. Altogether there were five hundred Rangers, more than ever before.

The Rangers were great scouts and spies, but the Army did not understand them. They did not wear uniforms. They all had broad brimmed hats and pointed-toed boots with high heels, but each man wore whatever clothes he wanted. The Rangers never drilled like regular soldiers and they did not even salute Colonel Hays. When there was fighting to be done, the Rangers were the best men to be found, but they did not like to sit around and wait. They hated Mexicans and were always doing things the regular army did not allow their soldiers to do.

There was one thing Colonel Hays had the army do for his men. He ordered one thousand Colt Revolvers so each Ranger could have two six-guns. There was a little problem in getting the guns. Colt's factory had closed because he had been unable to sell his guns to the army earlier. The army found him running a medicine show.

Hays sent Sam Walker to help Colt make some changes in the revolvers the Rangers had been using. The old guns had to be broken into three parts to be loaded. The new guns were heavier with a trigger guard and an easy way to load. The Rangers were delighted with this new model called the Walker-Colt revolver.

The army now wanted revolvers for its men so Sam Colt went into business again. He had helped the Rangers and they had returned the favor. Colt died a millionaire.

After the Mexican War the Rangers were disbanded. The Army was sent to protect the Indians on reservations and the Mexicans were supposed to be at peace with Texas. Since gold had been discovered in California, many Rangers, including Jack Hays, left Texas but there was still a need for them. The Indians were supposed to live on reservations but they still raided the settlers. The

Army was there to protect the Indians, not punish them outside the reservations.

It was then that Texans demanded that all Indians be sent out of the state. Even then the raids did not stop. Rip Ford was the new leader of the Rangers who were paid by the State of Texas. In 1859 Ford, with the help of some friendly Indians and his Rangers, went into Oklahoma. They attacked the Comanches living there and killed their chief, Iron Jacket, wearing his Spanish armor. The Rangers had no right to go outside Texas but they proved one thing. The Rangers could take the fight to the Comanches and beat them in their own land.

About the same time, Juan Cortinas was causing all sorts of trouble along the Rio Grande. The son of a fine family near Brownsville, one morning he was in town drinking coffee. One of his servants was arrested for being drunk and was mistreated by the sheriff. Cortinas objected to this and the sheriff made a bad remark to Cortinas. The Mexican then pulled out a gun, shot the sheriff and rode off with the servant on one horse. This made the Texans living in Brownsville very angry, but the Mexicans had enjoyed it.

The Texans said they were going after Cortinas, but they never did. However, Cortinas got a number of men from Mexico as well as his friends in Texas and rode into Brownsville. Very quickly he captured the city, killed three Americans, opened the jail and took Fort Brown, the army post. The Texans were helpless while Cortinas and his men looked for their enemies. As soon as Cortinas left, the Texans sent out calls for help.

For the next three months, Cortinas and his men staged a running battle with the Rangers and the army. There were losses on both sides, but at last on December 26, 1859, Cortinas' forces were unable to take any more. They crossed the river into Mexico and the "war" was over, but that was not the last to be heard from Cortinas.

Fifteen years later, Cortinas was still in Mexico but he was sending men into Texas to steal cattle. Indians from the West were attacking the people and trying to settle in that part of Texas. There were also many men in Texas who were attacking their neighbors and killing and robbing. It was time for the Rangers to act and they did.

Captain L.H. McNelly was put in charge of a Special Force of Texas Rangers. They were to look after the Mexican border and the Southwest. Cortinas' men were stealing cattle and horses and herding them near the mouth of the Rio Grande. McNelly and his Rangers trailed them to the Palo Alto Prairie where they killed every bandit. A few months later the Rangers fought at Las Cuevas. There were four hundred Mexicans to about for-

ty Rangers, but numbers never seemed to matter to the Texans. The Rangers killed sixteen bandits and McNelly even got the Mexicans to return the cattle they had stolen.

At the same time McNelly was in charge of Special Forces, Major John Jones was put in charge of the Frontier Batallion. Small groups of Rangers were placed along the western borders of settlements. They were to keep back the Indians, but most of their work was with white men. This was a time when robbers and murderers brought terror to the settlers. Often there were feuds and mobs to be quieted.

There were so many outlaws in Texas that a book was made with the names of the wanted men. A copy was given to every Ranger and he had plenty to read. There were over 3000 names. Among the most famous was John Wesley Hardin who had killed twenty-five or thirty men and Sam Bass, the train robber. You can be sure the Rangers knew those names well for they got both men.

By 1900 the work of the Rangers had

changed and the Frontier Batallion was ended. The Indians had been driven out, the mobs and feuds were no more and many of the robbers had been captured. Now the Rangers became more like police. There were sent to find out who might be breaking the law and to help catch the law breakers. There was a time when fence cutting caused much trouble.

Each Ranger was made an officer and given much the same duties as other peace officers with one difference. The Rangers were sent wherever there was trouble the local officers could not handle. There was still plenty for them to do. About 1910 there were revolutions in Mexico that worried the people along the border. During World War I spies tried to slip into the United States through Texas. Bootleggers and smugglers came to Texas during Prohibition. The oil boom brought many bad people to Texas.

Today there are still Texas Rangers. They are no longer required to "ride like a Mexican, trail like an Indian, shoot like a Tennessean and fight like the very devil." Yet every Ranger is just as carefully picked. Each man is trained in the latest ways of catching law breakers and in keeping the peace. Instead of a horse, the Ranger rides in a high powered car. He most likely uses a helicopter to trail a wanted man. He can shoot as well as any Tennessean, but he had rather catch his man. He is so soft spoken you might never think of him as a devil, but there is no man more to be feared by those who do wrong.

Texas has many things of which to be proud. It is a beautiful state filled with people who have brought honor and fame to its name. Among those must be listed the men known as the Texas Rangers.